Once Upon a Time

Ever After High™

Once Upon a Time

A STORY COLLECTION

BY SHANNON HALE

LITTLE, BROWN BOOKS FOR YOUNG READERS
www.lbkids.co.uk

LITTLE, BROWN BOOKS FOR YOUNG READERS

First published in the United States in 2014 by Little, Brown and Company
First published in Great Britain in 2015 by Little, Brown Books for Young Readers

3 5 7 9 10 8 6 4

A CIP catalogue record for this book
is available from the British Library.

ISBN 978-0-349-13202-0

Printed and bound by CPI Group (UK) Ltd, Croydon, CR0 4YY

The paper and board used in this book are
made from wood from responsible sources.

MIX
Paper from
responsible sources
FSC® C104740
www.fsc.org

Little, Brown Books for Young Readers,
an imprint of Hachette Children's Group,
published by Hodder and Stoughton Limited
338 Euston Road, London NW1 3BH

An Hachette UK Company
www.hachette.co.uk

www.lbkids.co.uk

For MariBelle and Oliviana,
who are masters of their own stories

A Map of the World of Ever After High

CONTENTS

INTRODUCTION

ONCE UPON A TIME...

In a land beyond imagination, there is a boarding school for the sons and daughters of the most famous fairytale characters who ever lived. All the students at the fablelous Ever After High are there to learn how to follow in their parents' footsteps, ensuring their stories will continue to be told.

The students' second year at Ever After High is known as their Legacy Year. Legacy Year students attend an important celebration known as Legacy Day, where they pledge to take the same paths as their parents.

They promise to follow their destinies by signing their names in an enchanted tome known as the Storybook of Legends.

The following stories take place just before a Legacy Year like no other begins, as a group of memorable students prepare to face their destinies....

Cedar Wood
(and the)
End of Summer

As soon as the sun was up, Cedar Wood was up, too. She didn't need much sleep. Or any, really. Night was a time to rest her imagination, not her wooden body. But this morning, Cedar had been alert for hours before dawn, just lying on her cot, watching the shadows shift on the ceiling, thinking and waiting. It was the last day of summer. Time for a new school year.

As soon as pale yellow light licked her curtains, she rose and crept downstairs. Her own knees creaked more than the stairs did. In the kitchen, she made herself a cup of willow sap tea and heated up a nice bowl of acorn porridge.

Morning sunlight gilded the edges of things, making the cozy cottage look as rich as a royal palace. Blocks of wood were stacked along the walls. The floor was carpeted with wood shavings, the tables busy with half-finished projects, the ceilings dangling puppets, dolls, flutes, wind chimes, and dozens of other carved wooden creations. Cedar took it all in, trying to paint a picture of home in her mind that might last her all year.

"Good morning," said Cedar's father, Pinocchio, as he came down the stairs. He kissed the top of Cedar's head and then busied himself buttering hot cross buns. He had warm brown skin like she did, still retaining the shade of the wood he'd once been carved from. But he was truly alive now. Real hair grew from his head, though his nose no longer did. It was a little bigger than average, retaining some memory of when it had lengthened with every lie.

"I thought we could finish those nesting dolls today," said Pinocchio. "You are so good at painting the eyes! And then tonight there's the end-of-summer clambake on the beach—"

"She's going today." Gepetto was on the stairs. He still had bedhead, his white hair standing straight up. His bottom lip lowered, pouting. "The fairy ferry sails after lunch. Isn't that right, my girl?"

Cedar nodded.

Pinocchio's smile dropped, but he picked it back up, showing Cedar a brave face. "I nearly forgot! She's off on another adventure, another year of school, to conquer evil and battle monsters and finish her thronework!"

He picked her up and danced her around. Cedar laughed. She was fairy, fairy excited to see Raven Queen, Madeline Hatter, and her other friends again, but the twinkle of sadness in her dad's eyes lingered.

All summer, she had worked alongside her father and grandfather, painting the dolls they carved, helping customers pick out the perfect gift or souvenir.

"My most helpful girl," her father would call her.

"My sapling, my acorn, my treasure," her grandfather would call her.

She had no heart, but her heartwood felt tender. She *would* miss home, but she would have all the wonders and friendships of Ever After High to distract her, while her family would still be in this little house, everything reminding them that Cedar was gone.

"I don't want you to be lonely," Cedar couldn't help saying. "Or hungry! You two always forget to go shopping till the cupboards are bare. I'll be right back." She grabbed some baskets and ran out of the house.

Old Mother Hubbard's Corner Market was always open early, so Cedar filled her baskets with Pinocchio's and Gepetto's favorite foods: bread, fruitcake, sardines, and humble pie.

She stocked the shelves and closed the cupboards at home in satisfaction but as she turned around, she still felt anxious about the quiet little house.

"I'll be back in a splinter!" she called out as she left again.

In the summer, her village was a major tourist destination, famous for the many artists who lived there. The main street was lined with white cottages like her own—families lived upstairs and worked downstairs. Through a window, she spotted the Shoemaker coming downstairs just as tiny elves scurried away, leaving beautiful shoes on the tabletop. Next door, a fairy godmother was stacking up bright orange and yellow gourds.

"Good morning, Cedar!"

"Good morning," Cedar replied with a happy wave.

For a fee, the fairy godmother would tap a gourd with her magic wand and turn it into a toy carriage right before your eyes. The tourists loved that.

The sweet smell of baking crust rolled under her nose from the Four-and-Twenty Blackbird Pie Shop, though Cedar knew for a fact that the pies were made from pumpkin, apple, or pomegranate meringue and *not* birds. If you bought a pie, stuck in your thumb, and pulled out a plum, you won a tinsel crown.

Across the street, Woodrow Wolf, a distant cousin of Mr. Badwolf, was hard at work. Huff and Puff Glass Blowers made cups, vases, and delicate glass flowers that looked comically tiny in his huge, hairy paws.

He waved and growled, "'Morning, Cedar. Off today?"

"Good morning, Woodrow. Keep an eye on the carvers for me, will you?"

He nodded but didn't smile. His teeth still upset some of the locals.

At the end of the main street, black-haired and pink-dressed She was selling seashells by the seashore.

"Hey, She!" Cedar called out, waving.

She waved back. "Hi, Cedar! Hey, how can a clam cram in a clean cream can?"

At her feet, a clam was doing just that.

Cedar shrugged. "The world is full of tongue-twisting wonders."

"But just one wooden wandering wonderer!" said She.

Cedar smiled but kept walking before she said out loud just how that made her feel. Her village was the best place in the world, filled with creative, interesting, and loving people. But sometimes Cedar still felt alone in a world of people nothing like her. *Just one wooden wandering wonderer. The only one.*

A carriage rumbled by her with twelve nearly identical children peering out of it, waving good-bye. Cedar waved back. The summer season was ending. Some tourists were taking a last breakfast in the outdoor cafés facing the ocean; others were cramming suitcases bulging with souvenirs into rental hybrid carriages to head back home. The village would become quiet. A little lonely.

Oberon and Titania's Flower Market smelled as if a bottle of perfume had exploded. Several tiny pixies buzzed around, breathing on the blooms and brightening their colors. Oberon hobbled over to Cedar. He was a tall, robust man, but had injured his leg in a fairy carriage race some years back. It didn't slow him down much, though.

"Good morning, Oberon!" Cedar said. "I need loads of the brightest, happiest flowers you have."

"What a lovely order," said Oberon. "Would you like to add on a perma-bloom spell?"

"Yes, please," said Cedar. She couldn't help blurting out an explanation. "I want them to last until I come home for winter break. I'm leaving today, you see, and I'm worried Dad and Grandpa will be lonely without me, so I'm hoping that flowers will help cheer them up."

"Oh, is it time already?" Titania clasped her hands to her chest, and Cedar could see her green thumb. It was literally green. Probably what made her so adept at growing flowers. "Summer always ends too quickly."

Titania began to sniffle as she picked out flowers, though Cedar wasn't sure if it was because of sadness at summer's end or just allergies. So awkward being a flower fairy with a pollen allergy.

At an adjacent outdoor café, two tourist boys dressed in swimming suits were gobbling up enough tea cakes to make any candy-housed witch well pleased. They eyed Cedar. She quickly looked away, but she couldn't help overhearing their whispers.

"Look, there's Cedar Wood."

"Who?"

"Cedar Wood. Pinocchio's daughter."

"Oh, that's nothing. Last year, I saw Apple White at a One Reflection concert."

"Hey!" The taller of the boys hopped over the railing from the café porch into the Flower Market. "Hey, Pinocchio's daughter! Tell a lie. We want to see your nose grow."

Cedar busied herself examining a bunch of hollyhocks. "My nose doesn't grow, and I can't tell a lie."

"Come on, just one." The tall boy held up his MirrorPhone and started snapping pictures. "I want to see it grow so I can show everyone back home."

"I told you, it doesn't grow," she said. She felt all redwood in the face even though she knew she couldn't actually blush like a real girl.

"Come on—"

"It doesn't grow! I'm not exactly like my dad. The Blue-Haired Fairy cursed me—or blessed me, or something—with caring and kindness *and* honesty after Dad carved me from magical wood, so I actually *cannot* tell a lie. I only speak the truth." She took a deep breath and muttered, "Whether I want to or not."

The boy smiled and nudged his friend. "Hey, she's magically bound to tell the truth! So, Cedar Wood, tell us what you think about your *dad*?"

"My dad? Well, he's kind and caring without needing a curse. I love him."

The boy frowned, as if he'd been hoping for more juicy gossip. But his frown turned up in a sneaky way that made Cedar feel loose in her joints.

"Tell us what it's like to be a fake puppet girl?" he asked.

"What? That's none of your business. And really

rude." She tried to stop there, but her mouth just kept going. "But I worry that no one sees me as a person. Sure, I can talk and think and imagine feelings and smells, almost like I'm real. But I'm not. And I want to be real so badly I'd brave a wood-chipper for the chance, but at the same time, the thought of signing the Storybook of Legends and promising to live out my dad's story scares me. I want to choose for myself what my life will be. I don't like being forced to tell the truth or become the next Pinocchio even if Pinocchio is a pretty good story, and I especially don't like having to tell you all this even though I don't want to. I wish I could shut up!"

The boy laughed.

"Hey, leave her alone, huh?" said the shorter boy, but his friend ignored him.

"Tell us more, Cedar Wood!" the tall boy demanded. "What are you most scared of?"

Cedar left her baskets of flowers and ran.

She spoke as she ran, still answering his question because she couldn't stop herself.

"Woodpeckers, wood-chippers, woodchucks, axes, fires, termites. Never turning real. Being stuck in a wooden body with an honesty curse forever. Disappointing my dad, letting my friends down…"

She finally stopped running when her feet sank into warm beach sand. The waves rolled up toward her, licking the sand and rushing back again. The sound calmed her. She sat, doing her best to not-think and not-feel for several minutes. She wished taking deep, slow breaths could help calm her like it did for real people.

Nearby, the Blue-Haired Fairy was wearing a hot-pink swimsuit and a gauzy cover-up, lounging on a beach chair and reading a thick novel titled *The Bloody End of the Trident*. Although her signature blue locks were hidden under a large sunhat, an ogre in a flowered shirt still recognized the famous fairy, sneaking up to snap a selfie with her on his MirrorPhone.

Cedar waited till he left before approaching. She sat on the sand, pulling her knees to her chest.

"Hey," Cedar said.

"No photos, please," the Blue-Haired Fairy said from behind her book.

"It's just me," said Cedar.

Sparkly blue magic lifted the book out of the way and laid it on the beach chair.

"Cedar, darling, you're still here!" said the fairy. "When does your fairy ferry leave dock?"

"This afternoon," said Cedar.

The fairy lowered her large, glamorous sunglasses and peered at Cedar's face. "Ah. You are *feeling* things today."

"I know they're not real…my feelings…." Cedar drew a circle in the sand with her finger. "I know I just imagine the feelings, since I'm made of wood and all, but they *feel* real…."

"It's your Legacy Year. You will sign the Story-book of Legends and promise to become the next Pinocchio, and yet you are unsure if that's what you want."

"I do know what I want. Well, I do know one thing. How much longer…?"

Cedar didn't finish the question, but the fairy understood. She pushed her glasses up and leaned back, seeming to relish the sunshine on her face.

"Patience, my darling. There can be no Happily Ever After unless the story comes first."

A single sparkle of blue magic traveled to Cedar's nose and lit upon it, buzzing like a bee. She went cross-eyed, looking at it. The sparkle lifted off, exploded into a blue flower before her face. Cedar smiled and tried to hold the flower, but it turned to smoke, drizzling through her fingers like sand.

"And a story is always filled with *conflict*, *danger*, and *uncertainty*!" The fairy spoke the disagreeable words the way some might say "cupcakes, swing sets, and balloon animals!"

"But when?" Cedar asked. "When will I become real like Dad?"

"By the wand, girl! You already know so much of your future; you must treat the unknown as precious. I'd no sooner spoil it for you than read the last page of a book first." Blue magic lifted the crime thriller and flipped it open to the last page. The fairy read: "'The tall, monocled Keith wiped the bread pudding off his beard and stuffed the red mask back into the pocket of his sleek, silk suit—' Wait, Keith was the Red Mask all along? I don't believe it!"

The Blue-Haired Fairy flipped back to the

middle, the book floating again before her face. She became so engrossed she didn't seem to hear the calls for help. In fact, no one did. The beach was so quiet, most tourists already gone home.

Cedar stood up, shielding her eyes from the sun. Way out in the surf, someone was splashing.

Out of the water ran the shorter of the boys she'd seen back at the Flower Market.

"My friend!" he said, trying to catch his breath. "His foot caught on some kelp."

Cedar ran forward. She could make out the tall boy's head, his arms rising up and slapping down against the water's surface in a panicked flail.

"I tried to help him," said the shorter boy, "but I can't swim."

"I can swim," said Cedar.

Not only that, but she could also float. Being made of wood had some advantages.

Cedar threw off her shoes, ran into the surf, dived under a wave, and swam. The foam splashed against her face and the water was chilly, but cold never bothered her.

She passed the buoy that warned NO SWIMMING: KELP FOREST and reached the boy. His face was tilted up, his neck submerged. His breath was wet and desperate.

Cedar dived underwater. Her wooden body wanted to float back up, but she clung to a branch of kelp and pulled herself down. Finding the kelp that wrapped around the boy's ankle, she cut through it with the small knife she always kept in her art kit in her pocket. Just a few minutes ago she had wished she could breathe and take deep breaths just like everyone else. She was glad now that wish hadn't come true.

She swam beneath him, balancing his back against hers, and kicked to shore. His friend waded into the surf and helped her drag the tall boy onto the sand. While he gasped for breath, Cedar wrung the seawater from her dress and tightened the brass pegs at her elbows and knees.

Finally, the half-drowned boy looked up. His eyes widened. "You!"

Cedar wrinkled her nose. "Me. The one you were cruel to earlier."

"So . . . so why did you save me?"

"Because I'm not only honest, I'm also caring and kind. You're a bully, but you can change. One day

I'm going to change into a real girl. You don't have to wait for the Blue-Haired Fairy's magic. Be a real boy. Start using your heart now!"

Cedar worried that she sounded like a teacher scolding a naughty student, but then she chose not to worry anymore. She just turned and marched away.

At the Flower Market, Titania and Oberon had her overflowing baskets waiting. She spent the rest of the morning decorating the house with bright, fragrant fairy flowers and helping her dad sell puppets to the last of that season's customers.

So much was uncertain in her future, but she had a father and a grandfather at home, good friends waiting at school, and no strings to hold her back.

Somehow, Cedar knew that all would be right in The End.

Apple White
(and the)
Ebony-Haired Legacy

APPLE WHITE OPENED THE PINK SILK curtains even wider to let in all that buttery sunshine.

"My, what a perfect day for travel!" she said.

Her bedroom was bustling with servants in matching white uniforms, dwarves running errands, and friendly woodland creatures.

A robin hovered before Apple, a red slipper in its beak. It cocked its head to one side as if asking a question.

"Yes, pack that one," said Apple. "In fact, let's just pack all my shoes, shall we?"

The squirrels rustling across the floor squeaked in unison. They began carrying shoes from the closet and depositing them in an open trunk as if storing nuts for the winter.

"Not the blue ones," Apple called to a bluebird in her sock drawer. "The white ones, if you please!"

Apple's MirrorPhone played a measure of One Reflection's single "You Don't Know You're Charming" to announce she'd received another hext message. This one was from Briar Beauty. Apple typed with one hand while brushing her blond curls with the other. Her hair never seemed to need brushing, but she was an overachiever.

BRIAR: Apple! When will you get to Ever After High?

APPLE: My father is prepping the Hybrid Carriage now. I should be there in a few short hours.

BRIAR: Hexcellent. Am planning a Book-to-School party. Going to be a page ripper!!!

APPLE: I'm there. Charm you later!

"Snoozy! Snappy!" Apple called to her dwarf lackeys. "The first four trunks are ready to go. Would you be so kind as to carry them down? You, too, Pouty— don't you stick out that bottom lip, you silly."

"My name's not Pouty," Frank said poutily.

"Careful with that end, Sloppy!" Apple said cheerily.

"My name is Phil," Sloppy grumbled.

Apple laughed. "You sillies!"

She patted their heads, and they couldn't help but smile. Who could hold back a smile when looking at Apple White?

The sounds of cheering floated in through her window. Apple stepped onto her balcony, and the cheering grew louder. In the courtyard below, hundreds of men, women, and children from the village had gathered, many wearing I ♥ APPLE T-shirts.

"My dear subjects, you are simply, unquestionably perfect!" she called out, tossing candy and coins to the crowd. She kept a candy-and-coin basket on the balcony so she would be ready for adoring crowds at a moment's notice.

"No, *you* are perfect!" someone shouted, and the cheering renewed.

She pressed her hand to her heart. The whole world was so perfectly splendid she could just burst!

Above Apple, some birds carried a long pink ribbon in their beaks. A message was stitched across the satin ribbon: WE LOVE YOU, APPLE! EMBRACE YOUR DESTINY!

Destiny. She was beginning her Legacy Year, the first step in the journey to achieve her own Happily Ever After. Apple could hardly wait.

Apple strode down to the courtyard, where her parents waited like a portrait of the ideal king and queen. Her mother's black hair was curled under her golden crown. Her skin was still white as snow, her lips red as blood. She was as beautiful now as she had been when a magic mirror had named her the Fairest One of All.

Apple's father stood beside his wife, one hand on his sword hilt, always ready to do battle—though, of course, he'd never actually done any battle. His claim to fame had been falling in love with a comatose girl inside a glass coffin. But he looked so regal with a sword.

"This is a royally important year," said her mother as she helped Apple into the Hybrid Carriage. Her voice was high and a little squeaky, as if all that time spent lost in the woods with squirrels had taken its toll. "I am so proud of you. I know you will prepare yourself to be the perfect Snow White."

The maids, servants, guards, and dwarves in the huge Hybrid Carriage all nodded. Apple blushed. They must have noticed how dedicated she was to her subjects, how hard she had been studying Kingdom Management, all the time she put into preparing to be a queen—

"Just look at her eyes, her skin," whispered one of her maids.

"I did not think it possible," a groomsman whispered back, "but she is becoming even more beautiful than her mother."

"So beautiful," said a manservant. "The *perfect* Snow White."

"Well, except for the hair. A shame she was born blond."

Apple winced.

"I think her blond hair is even lovelier than her mother's black hair."

"How can you? The fairytale specifies 'hair like ebony'—"

"Listen, the hair doesn't matter. Her eyes, her nose, those lips, that profile! She is the definition of beauty."

Apple turned her face to the window as the Hybrid Carriage started on its way. Was that all everyone saw in her? A perfect profile? A beauty like her mother? Surely being Snow White meant more than just looking pretty and having black hair.

Legacy Year would be *her* year. The beginning to her story. But she didn't just want to prove that she was pretty enough to be a queen, black hair or blond. She wanted to prove she could rule like one.

From the Desk of
Apple White

ONE REFLECTION

WAKE THE GNOME

ONE REFLECTION
WAKE THE GNOME

TRACKS:
You Don't Know You're Charming
Tell Me a Lie, Pinocchio
Little Things (Thumbelina's Song)
Losing Your Destiny
Rock Me, Rockabye Baby
Kiss You Awake
Narrator, Tell the Story of My Life
Best Song Ever After
Midnight Memories (Cinderella's Song)
Don't Forget the Setting Where You Belong
Strung: A Puppet Ballad

Raven Queen
(and the)
Mirror Prison

NCE UPON A NEW SCHOOL YEAR, RAVEN Queen was packing. She blasted Tailor Quick's new album from her MirrorPod, dancing while grabbing things from her closet and tossing them into her clothing trunk. The heap of clothes was entirely purple and black, so she threw in a pair of silver sandals to add color.

Raven opened her window. The sun was setting into the copper sea. The last page of summer was closing.

"Hey, Ooglot!" she called out as she hefted her trunk onto the windowsill of her fourth-story bedroom. She let the trunk fall. In the courtyard below, the family ogre caught it with one blue hand and waved to her. She waved back.

Summer had been nice. No homework—just hours and hours to listen to music and read adventure novels. A couple of days each week she had babysat Cook's twin boys—Butternut and Pie—in exchange for heaps of pastries. And she and Dad had sailed their little boat down the coast to spend a week with Pinocchio and his daughter, Cedar Wood. Raven had loved making tea visits with the Blue-Haired Fairy, playing card games by the fire, and staying up late with Cedar, singing karaoke and laughing into their pillows.

All nice as mice. But Raven was eager to rejoin her friends at Ever After High for her second year of boarding school.

She was trying very hard not to think about how her Legacy Day was just a few weeks away. Ever since witnessing Legacy Day as a first-year, she'd done her best to block it out. Back then, the future had seemed so distant.

A foghorn bellowed, calling her to dinner.

Raven put on a sweater as she left her room. Queen Castle was chilly. There were far too many unoccupied rooms to bother lighting fires in all their hearths. When her mother had ruled, the castle had teemed with servants, soldiers, and creatures of the shadows. And all of them had watched young Raven, ready to tattle to her mother if they caught Raven doing anything kind.

"Raven," her mother would say, "Yop the Goblin says he saw you apologize to a rat for stepping on its tail. Such behavior must stop!"

"But I didn't mean to step on its tail," she'd say.

"Not that. The apology! The Evil Queen never apologizes for anything. You must learn that now."

Raven preferred the castle mostly empty.

She made her way through the massive Great Hall, feeling as if she'd been swallowed by a whale. She stuck out her tongue at the shadows and slid down the banister of the staircase as she used to when she was a kid.

She flung open the huge dining room doors and announced, "I'm here!" Years ago her mother used to host hundreds of guests at that dining table. Tonight, as usual, the only diners were Raven, her father, Cook, and Cook's four-year-old sons.

"Raven!" Butternut and Pie said in unison. They had hair as orange as Butternut's namesake and faces as round as Pie's.

"Hey, little Cooklings," she said.

"I made this for you," said Pie, pushing a piece of paper across the table. Raven held up a finger painting of herself done in all black and purple.

"Wicked cool. Thank you," she said.

Raven's father, the Good King, kissed her forehead when she sat beside him. His trimmed beard was beginning to gray, and the top of his head was totally bald, as if his hair had made room for the golden crown he rarely bothered to wear. His eyes were bright blue and brightened even more when he smiled—which was often.

"All packed?" he asked. "Don't forget a warm coat. And rain boots. And an enchanted umbrella."

"Got it," said Raven. "And don't you stay cooped up in here all year without me. Cook, make sure he gets outside, goes sailing and fishing."

"Of course. Now dinner. I made roast duck," Cook said hopefully, lifting up the platter.

"I'll just have a princess pea–butter sandwich, please," Raven said while playing peekaboo behind her napkin with Butternut.

Cook rolled her eyes but handed Raven her usual sandwich.

"Thank you," Raven said, and then winced automatically. But her mother wasn't there to scold her for being nice.

Her father must have noticed her wince, because he put a comforting hand on her shoulder and smiled.

"My meat is cold," said Butternut.

"I can warm it up for you," Raven said, wiggling her fingers as if preparing to cast a spell.

"No!" both Cook and the king said at once, lunging to their feet.

Raven laughed.

"Oh my, you had me for a moment." The king pressed his hand to his heart and sat back down.

A couple of years before, Raven had tried to reheat her father's meal and ended up setting the entire table on fire. She wouldn't make that mistake again. Dark magic + good intentions = catastrophe.

After the plum pudding, the Good King said, "Cook, thank you so much for a perfect dinner.

Raven, would you...?" He inclined his head toward the door.

Raven's stomach turned cold, but she followed him out.

Once they were alone in the hall, he whispered, "It's time, Raven. If you'd rather not..."

"No, I'll go talk to her."

"I'll go with you," he said.

Raven shook her head. She was fifteen now. She was old enough to face her mother alone.

Raven straightened her shoulders and began the long walk to the Queen's Wing in the Other Side of the Castle for the first time in a year. Colors dimmed—dark wood walls, scarlet and black carpets. Portrait paintings looked down. Her mother smiling. Her mother not smiling. Her mother's profile. A close-up of her mother's nose. In one, her mother was winking. In all of them, she was beautiful.

Monstrous statues seemed to watch Raven as she passed. Drapes rustled where there was no draft. Raven's forehead prickled with cold sweat.

Two guards in shiny armor stood outside her mother's old bedroom, wielding spiky spears and magic staffs. They nodded to her as she opened the door.

"Remember," said one, "never touch the mirror."

"I remember," she said.

The room was so thick with cobwebs it seemed as if skeletons had decorated for a party. Raven fought her way through the webs to the far wall and ripped the velvet cloth off the mirror. She saw her own reflection staring back—long black hair with purple highlights, dark eyebrows, strong nose and chin. It was strange to see her own face. She usually avoided looking at herself in mirrors. Mirror-gazing had been her mother's hobby.

"Mirror, mirror on the wall," she said, "um…show me my mother."

The mirror didn't require a rhyme to work. Rhyming was *so* last chapter.

The mirror sparked, electricity skating across its silver surface. Slowly her mother appeared. She was wearing a striped jumpsuit. Her dark hair was piled on her head in the shape of a crown.

"Raven, is that you? You're so…so beautiful!" The Evil Queen laughed. "You *are* going to give that fair-skinned, blood-lipped brat a run for her money!"

Raven pulled her hair out from behind her ear, letting it fall over half her face.

"Hey, Mom," she said. "How's, you know, mirror prison?"

"Meh," the Evil Queen said with a pretty shrug. "Tell me all the gossip. What's happening in Ever After? Did they figure out how to undo my poisoning of Wonderland madness yet? Has someone else copied me and tried to take over all the kingdoms? Is your father still a mind-numbing excuse for a man?"

Raven clenched her fists. *Don't make fun of my dad!* she wanted to shout. But she met those dark eyes in the mirror, took a deep breath, and looked down. Even with her mother imprisoned far away, she didn't dare argue back. "Everything's pretty much the same as last year. And the year before."

"Ha! See what happens when I'm gone? *Nothing*. I made life interesting. I hope you learn from this, darling. You have to go out there and force life to be what you want it to be, like I did."

"Yeah," said Raven. Her mother had certainly made her childhood interesting. In those days, the castle was always crowded with soldiers in spiked armor and creatures that scurried through shadows and hissed at her. Quality time with Mother had included sitting on her lap while the queen met with her generals and hatched plots to kill, conquer, and rule, or spending hours in the dungeon workshop, coughing on smoke and helping Mother make toxic potions and evil spells.

"So are you ready for your Legacy Year?" asked the queen. "Ready to sign the Storybook of Legends and bind yourself to following in my footsteps?"

Raven shrugged.

"You should be eager to become the next Evil Queen. Why, your legacy is one of power, control, and command! Just think, you could have been born to one of those pathetic princesses who have to sit in a tower and wait to be rescued. Or worse, get suckered into eating a poisoned apple."

The queen cackled beautifully. If ever a cackle could bring a tear to your eye, it was the Evil Queen's.

"I guess I just... I just..."

"What? Don't mumble. Stop slouching and speak up like a queen. Now, what were you saying?"

Raven straightened her spine. "Nothing. Never mind."

"Don't be so timid, Raven. This is your chance to show those dull 'good' folk just what you're made of!"

"Okay, I'll try." And as a show of effort, she cracked a small smile.

"I'm so proud! Oh, I miss you, my beautiful baby girl." Her mother lifted her hand, pressing it against the mirror as if she were just on the other side of a window. "Let me touch you, even if it's only through glass."

Raven's hand lifted, almost of its own accord. Her mother really did love her, in her way. Hope was like a sticky, too-sweet syrup she yearned to drink just one more time. But Raven stopped her hand before she touched the mirror. This wasn't the actual mirror prison. That was far away and locked up tight. But her mother was such a powerful sorceress, she might be able to take Raven's hand even through a viewing portal.

"I love you, Mother," said Raven, "but I'm not helping you escape."

The queen's eyes narrowed, and her hand dropped. "*Hmph.* If you were as evil as I raised you to be, you wouldn't hesitate. I must say, Raven Queen, I'm disappointed in you. Never mind. I'll watch with interest to see what you accomplish. You have inherited a bottomless capacity for true evil and breathtaking power. Don't waste it." She leaned so close all Raven could see in the mirror were her mother's deep purple eyes. "Give 'em hex, Raven."

Raven swallowed. All she wanted was to run away.

Their time ended and the mirror turned off. Instead of her mother's face, Raven saw her own again. It was remarkable, really, how much they looked alike.

Briar Beauty
(and the)
Jewelry Thieves

Briar Beauty did not take packing lightly.

In her huge bedroom, she had twelve mannequins made from woven, de-thorned briar branches. She'd dressed them again and again, mixing tops and bottoms, and adding and taking away tiaras and belts. From crownglasses to shoes, she needed to plan out each outfit she would take with her to boarding school. After all, this was her Legacy Year, the year she would seal her destiny to become the next Sleeping Beauty. Hers was a fairy, fairy important story; all eyes would be on Briar. And she really needed to look her best.

Briar took a step back to look over her creations. Her stomach fluttered nervously. Something was still missing. She dialed her best friends forever after, Apple White and Blondie Lockes, for a MirrorChat.

"Girls! You're looking fairest, as always," said Briar. "How have you been?" Briar hadn't seen her friends in two months, since their early-summer trip to Looking Glass Beach.

"I'm so excited for our Legacy Year!" said Apple. "I'm sure the hexcitement is brightening my eyes and putting a glow in my cheeks."

"Totally. But I need your help. What do you think about these?" Briar asked, holding up her Mirror-Pad to the clothed briar-branch mannequins.

"Spellbinding," said Apple.

"They are just right!" said Blondie.

"What jewelry will you use to accessorize?" Apple asked.

"Jewelry! Thank you! That's exactly what they're missing! I'll call you back. The end," said Briar.

"The end," said Apple and Blondie, hanging up.

Briar pulled out her jewelry box from under her bed. Well, it was more of a jewelry trunk. Dashing young men were always giving her necklaces and bangles. One of the many benefits of being a princess.

Briar opened the lid. The trunk was empty.

She gasped.

"Mom!" she yelled. "Mom! We've been robbed! Mom! Get up here!"

No answer. Well, that was no surprise. Spending one hundred years in a magical slumber had some side effects, and Sleeping Beauty was known to doze off. Frequently. Briar just hoped her mother hadn't fallen asleep anywhere inconvenient again. Like into her morning porridge.

Briar stepped out onto her windowsill. Jumping was the fastest way to get downstairs, not to mention a total rush. But it wasn't until she was teetering on the edge of the sill that she noticed that the hay wagon—which was *always* right there—was *not* right there. Nothing below her but a hard cobblestone courtyard.

"Aah!" Briar said, her high-heeled shoes slipping. She gripped the curtains.

And then the worst thing possible happened. She got that familiar yawning feeling behind her eyes. The sensation was almost like the start of a sneeze, but she knew it wasn't a sneeze because this cursed thing happened to her several times a day. Apparently her mother's dozing thing was genetic.

"Help!" Briar yelled. "Hel—"

She fell asleep.

She seemed to lose consciousness for only a split second, but when she awoke she was no longer hanging out her window. She was in the courtyard below, thankfully in her father's arms. He must have caught her just in time.

"Briar!" he said. "How many times have I told you—"

"But the hay wagon—"

"…not to jump out of—"

"…is always right there, and—"

"…windows when you have a habit of—"

"…I've been robbed!"

"What?" Her father put her down so that he could place his fists on his hips and strike a hero's pose. He might be a middle-aged king now, but he had once been the brave young prince who battled his way into Sleeping Beauty's palace. And he *never* forgot that.

"Who would dare attack us here in our cozy home?" he said, gesturing to the enormous pink marble palace. "I won't rest until I find the villains!"

He ran off.

"It was my jewelry!" Briar shouted after his father because he'd forgotten to ask what was stolen. Her father was more likely to go find some dragon to battle than locate her stolen jewelry. How in Ever After could she maintain her fashion-forward status without any jewelry? This was an epic fairy-fail!

"Mom!" she shouted.

Briar started toward the ballroom and was knocked down by three of her little brothers running past.

"Hey!" she said.

But they just kept running.

Entering the ballroom, Briar realized her brothers had had a very busy morning. About a hundred dining room chairs were stacked in teetering towers and draped with sheets and blankets. Briar doubted there was a bed left in the palace that hadn't been stripped.

"Mom! Where are you? We've been robbed!"

In the far corner, one of the blanket fort's chair towers crashed to the floor. Two more brothers had pulled the sheets off those chairs, and they ran off, dragging the sheets behind them. Could her brothers have taken her jewelry? No, they had no use for trinkets. Besides, they seemed too busy with their blanket fort to bother with necklaces.

"Mom!"

Briar ran into the east gallery and grabbed hold of the zip line that was bolted to the ceiling. With a running start, she pushed off, zooming through the east gallery and the blue drawing room. Three more of her little brothers went swooshing by on a zip line going the other direction. Their arms were full of something black, and the music master was hollering and chasing after them—on foot. Briar shook her head. He'd never catch them.

"Where's Mom?" she yelled after her brothers. "And have you seen any robbers?"

But they were gone.

The zip line shot her through the yellow drawing room and into the music room. There were lots of long corridors and connected rooms in the palace, so zip lines just made sense. Anyway, they were a blast to ride. Briar let go, landing on pillows on the music room floor.

Pillows lay scattered all over, ready in case the queen or her daughter passed out without warning. But her mother wasn't snoring on any of these cushions, and there was still no sign of robbers. What was going on?

Briar's stomach squeaked. She'd been too nervous about packing to eat breakfast.

"Mom! Where—"

Briar heard a snore. She ran toward the west breakfast room, her high heels clicking on the marble floors. Briar was skilled at running in heels. In fact, she was so used to high-heeled shoes that in the rare moments when she was barefoot, she walked on her toes.

"Oh, Mom," she said.

The brown-haired Beauty was sitting at the table, facedown in a plate of cold scrambled eggs, sleeping contentedly. Briar supposed eggs were less messy than porridge. She took off her sweater and draped it over her mother's shoulders in case she was cold.

And for a split second, Briar's heart pricked with an unusual sadness. At the grand Legacy Day ceremony that fall, Briar would sign the Storybook of Legends and magically bind herself to be the next Sleeping Beauty. Which meant she would have to sleep for *one hundred years*. Just think of all the parties she'd miss, all the years lost with her family and Apple and Blondie. Not to mention by the time she woke up, she'd be fashion backward!

Her mother snored. She did look cozy there, so content, so sleepy....

Oh no. There was that yawning feeling behind her eyes again. Briar slapped her cheeks.

"Don't fall asleep, don't fall asleep...."

She hit the floor pillows.

Briar's spontaneous napping was a major curse, but it did have one magical advantage. As she fell deeper asleep, conversations from all around the palace and grounds began to flow through her mind like vivid dreams.

"That sheep boy is cuckoo for the milkmaid. Have you noticed?" the cook asked one of the scrub girls. "Mooning about whenever she's near..."

"Fred's not really sick," one guard whispered to

another. "He's just sleepy. He was up late painting a self-portrait to send to his girlfriend…."

"I have more buried treasure!" her little brother Loyalty yelled, running into the rose garden, his hands full of—

Briar woke up with a start. *Aha!* She jumped to her feet.

"Briar?" said her mother, sitting up and picking chunks of scrambled egg off her cheek. "I think I dozed off. Where are the boys? I hope they haven't made a mess."

"Don't worry, Mom. I'll take care of it."

Briar raced to the second-floor conservatory, grabbed a zip-line handle, and flew out the window. She zipped over the courtyard and into the rose garden, landing on a feather mattress strategically placed by the fountain.

Sure enough, there was the missing hay wagon. Sheets and blankets were nailed up like sails. A black flag painted with a white skull and crossbones flew from the curtain-rod mast.

Apparently her brothers had abandoned the blanket fort and moved on to a new game. Seven of them were standing atop their hay-wagon pirate ship wearing strips of the music master's black robes tied over their heads like scarves and covering one eye. They waved wooden swords and yelled at the eighth brother, Tenacity, who was dressed all in green and perched atop the stone mermaid in the fountain. Tenacity must have lost the draw. It was always more fun to be a pirate.

Three identical brothers shouted up to Tenacity:

"We'll get you yet, Peter Pan!"

"How dare ye attack the good ship *Jolly Roger*!"

"We'll make Peter Pan pie out of ye!"

"Hey!" said Briar.

The triplets startled, staring at her with their uncovered brown eyes.

"The hay wagon?" she said. "And the sheets? And the music master's robes? Not to mention my jewelry!" She pointed to a recently uprooted rose-bush. She would bet her new black satin wedges that these little pirates had buried her jewelry there. "You little thieves! How could you? You know I leave for Ever After High tomorrow."

The boys nodded. They did know. And they didn't seem happy about it.

"Sorry, Briar," they said in unison.

Courage was holding the pirate flag, but he let it droop. Gallantry's lower lip trembled. Tenacity climbed down from the statue, getting his feet wet. Honor, the littlest one, sniffed.

Aw... They were as cute as a nest of summer-brown bunnies. Briar couldn't stay mad.

"Dig up my treasure, you pirates," she said, "or I'll have you walk the plank into crocodile-infested waters and show no mercy!"

"Yes, Briar," they said, starting to smile.

"That's Captain Hook to you, laddies!"

"Yes, Captain Hook!" the boys shouted, eyes bright.

"Now dig, ye scurvy grubs!" she said, tying one of the black strips over her own hair. "As soon as your captain has her treasure, we're off to invade the kitchens!"

The boys raised their wooden swords and gave her a hearty cheer.

Briar still had a lot of outfit planning and packing to do, but there was always time for a quick pirate party.

From the Desk of
Briar Beauty

Spelltacular Party Ideas

Book-to-School Party

Legacy Day Dance

Tea Tuesdays

~~Shin Splints Shindig~~

Litter Awareness Luncheon

Hairdo To-Do ← (talk to Poppy O'Hair)

~~Festival of Feet~~

The Spin Dizzy Riot and Cheese Sampler

The Crownculus Class Hyperbolic Frolic

Silly Walk Hop

Bunny Hop Bop

Carousel Carousal

Super-Secret Public Dance Party

Barber Barbecue ← (No actual barbers harmed)

My Favorite Furry Friend Function
← (too exclusive?)

The Pretend-You-Are-a-Duck Party

Herder History Party ⤶ (both sheep and cows?)

Corned Beef Hash Bash

In-Case-of-Giant-Butterfly-Attack Soiree

La Siesta Fiesta ⤶ (a snooze fest?)

The Tiara-Thalon Sweat-Together
Get-Together

Celery Celebration! ⤶ (who doesn't love celery?)

Giant Pumpkin Carving and Urban
Housing Gathering

The On-Time-to-Class Blast

The Glass Slipper Page Ripper
↳ (talk to Ashlynn)

Elf and Dwarf Team-Building Event

Reception for All Millers' Daughters,
Third Sons, and Helpful Beggars

Madeline Hatter

(and the)

Upside-Down Day

ADELINE HATTER WAS IN THE ENCHANTED Forest by sunrise, the best time of day to find charm blossoms. The vibrant pink flowers bloomed only in the morning, twirling on their stems toward the rising sun. Maddie added a few to her basket of wild peppermint, chamomile flowers, and dragon scales. A white rabbit paused nearby, sniffing some clover.

"How are you this sunny, shiny morning?" Maddie asked.

The rabbit sniffled and hopped away without a

word. Maddie shook her head. The rabbits of Ever After were just so impolite! Not even a "how do you do" or an "I'm late! I must be hopping!" And since leaving Wonderland, Maddie had yet to see a single rabbit wearing so much as a bow tie. Rabbits looked practically naked without bow ties.

Curiouser and curiouser. Maddie supposed she would never totally understand this nonsensical world outside Wonderland.

She hurried out of the forest, across the footbridge, around the grounds of Ever After High, and back into the Village of Book End. After a lazy summer, the main street of Book End was positively crowded. Tomorrow began a new school year at Ever After High, a boarding school for the teenage sons and daughters of fairytales. The first-year students arrived a day early in order to shop for clothes at the Gingerbread Boutique, shoes at the Glass Slipper, and MirrorPhones and MirrorPads at the Mirror Store. They wandered in groups or in pairs, but a few walked alone.

Just a year ago, Maddie had been one of the alone ones. Although she'd arrived in Book End with her father, a great deal of hats, and her pet dormouse, Earl Grey, she'd felt the absence of a good friend.

She checked her watch.

"Twenty-two hours, forty-seven minutes, and eighteen seconds to go!" she said to herself. Not long until her best friends till The End, Raven Queen and Cedar Wood, would return to Ever After High. At last! They both lived far, far away, and calls on the MirrorPhone just weren't the same as a friend by your side.

Maddie tried to turn the absence of her friends into something positive—missing them made her even more excited to start her second year!

The second year was Legacy Year—when the students would sign the Storybook of Legends and magically bind themselves to reliving their parents' fairytales. Maddie couldn't wait. Who wouldn't want to follow in her father's hat-tastic footsteps?

When Maddie opened the door to the Mad Hatter of Wonderland's Haberdashery & Tea Shoppe, a hiss of steam escaped, smelling of sugarplum biscuits and hot sweet tea. The place was crowded with first-year students taking a break from shopping. Teapots rattled and whistled on every table, creating a kind of music that made Maddie want to throw off her shoes and dance.

But first, she removed her tiny teacup hat and put on a basket hat bursting with live flowers. The price tag dangled rakishly over her forehead. She and her dad had made it a rule to always wear the merchandise.

Doors of different sizes and colors climbed up all the walls. A bright yellow door on the ceiling opened, and her father leaned down. While Maddie's mint-green hair was streaked with purple around her face, her father's was mint green streaked with white. Even upside down, his huge orange polka-dotted top hat remained firmly on his large head.

"Success?" asked the Mad Hatter.

Maddie nodded, holding up her basket of flowers and scales.

"Tea-riffic," he said.

He fell out the door, landing on a huge cushion on the floor. He hopped up and, in his stockinged feet, leaped like a gazelle through the shop and into the kitchen. Maddie was about to follow when a girl beside her said, "*Excuse* me."

Her hair was red, and her cheeks were dusted with light brown freckles. She had a mouth that seemed to want to smile, but for some reason her lips were tight. "I have been standing here for two entire minutes waiting for a seat."

"Oh!" said Maddie. "I'm so sorry. I think there's been some kind of misunderstanding." She leaned closer and whispered helpfully, "The seats here don't come to you. You have to walk over to them."

The girl's mouth gaped as if she was insulted. Maddie nodded sympathetically.

"I agree," Maddie said. "I've often thought that chairs that come to you are a hexcellent idea. Alas, it can't be helped. Ever After chairs have four good legs, but they just refuse to use them!"

The girl sputtered, "I don't know what you're talking about."

"I feel the same way all the time!" said Maddie. "Especially on an upside-down kind of day like today. It's a last day and also a first day—last day of summer, your first day in Book End. Last day before school starts, first day of a new chapter. It's enough to make a girl feel like she's sitting on her head!"

Again, the girl seemed to want to smile but didn't. Maddie wondered what possible reason anyone could have for holding back a smile.

"If you haven't the manners to show me to a seat, I'll do it myself." With a huff, the girl stalked over to an unoccupied table and yelled back to Maddie, "I want a cup of tea!"

"Tea-riffic!" said Maddie. "Dad has some lovely brews pipping and piping today—spritzle-fizzle tea, milkflower tea, chocolate-rhubarb-pumpkin-raspberry-dragon-fire tea—"

"Regular tea," said the girl. "That's what I drink at home, so that's what I'll have here."

"But—"

"I'm Clara Lear, you know."

Maddie stared blankly.

Clara Lear sighed. "Why doesn't anyone know my tale? My father is King Lear, and one day I'll be queen, so bring me what I ordered!"

"Er...regular tea isn't the sort of thing we brew," said Maddie. "Why, in Wonderland, the very idea of regular tea would make people laugh and laugh for days!"

Maddie smiled. Clara Lear did not.

"*Are* we in Wonderland?" Clara asked.

The question shocked Maddie into silence.

"I didn't think so," said Clara. "And a good thing, too. From what I know of Wonderland, it's just a kingdom full of nonsense and singing and uselessness. If you don't brew regular tea in Wonderland, then that's definitely the kind I want."

Maddie just nodded and left, trying not to think too much about the horrible things Clara had said about her home.

Just like in the shop, the walls in the kitchen were covered with doors. The tea cupboard door was painted as pink as an elephant and was just as large. But the moment Maddie put her hand on the knob, the cupboard shrank to book-size.

"There it goes again, Dad!" she called.

"What, is that teakettle singing?" he called back from inside a copper door. "I'm certain there's just something inside it. Possibly a singing ferret. Or a singing bat. But definitely something that sings."

"No, the tea cupboard is shrinking."

"Ah, yes," said the Mad Hatter. He emerged from the copper door, two jars of honey in his arms. A few fat bees buzzed around his head. "Having another identity crisis. I can understand that. Is it a cup? Or a board? Excellent questions, both!"

Maddie opened the cupboard door and reached in her hand. She seemed to remember spying a packet of regular tea in the back of the cupboard once, but her arm wasn't long enough to reach. Arms could be inconveniently short at times. So much trouble for regular tea!

Her father squinted down at the cupboard through his glasses.

"Can you manage to get inside it, Maddie, my girl?"

"I think I could almost get my head in," said Maddie.

"Wonderlandiful!" said her father.

"Of course, my head won't be much use without my shoulders."

"And the rest of you, too, I suppose. Yes, you're right. Having this and that attached to our heads does complicate things."

Then her father did something extraordinary.

Maddie laughed. "You frowned!" she said.

Her father snickered. "I did, didn't I? What an upside-down day."

So they both went over to the mirror on the wall, frowning and laughing at themselves and then trying to frown again. It was an excellent game, but it was soon interrupted by Clara shouting from her table.

"If I can't get any service here, I'll just give up on tea altogether and go elsewhere!"

Give up on tea? *Give up on tea?* Maddie had never heard of such a ridiculous idea in her life.

"Earl Grey!" Maddie called.

Her pet dormouse stuck his head out of a kettle, where he had been humming "Twinkle, Twinkle, Little Shrew."

"Earl Grey, you sweetie little mousey, you, will you go on a bold and brave mouse quest?"

Moments later Earl Grey returned from inside the cupboard (which was neither a cup nor a board) triumphant, with a packet of tea in his paws.

"Thank you, Sir Mouse!" she said. He solemnly removed his top hat and bowed, and Maddie knighted him by touching each of his furry shoulders with a teaspoon. Earl Grey liked to be knighted exactly six times each day.

Maddie tore open the paper packet of regular

tea and looked at the sad gray bag. It smelled like dirt. And not even nice, warm brown dirt full of fat, healthy worms and interesting bits of sparkly stones. No, like dusty dirt, the kind that was good for nothing but sweeping away.

Maddie frowned even though she wasn't looking in a mirror. This couldn't be what Clara Lear honestly wanted—or needed.

Maddie peeked through the kitchen door. All the tables were filled with groups of kids talking and laughing. But Clara sat alone, back stiff, eyes straight ahead. Maddie remembered her own loneliness before meeting Raven and Cedar. Just thinking about her friends made Maddie smile.

And suddenly she understood Clara Lear's tight lips. Maddie dropped the regular tea in the dustbin and went to fetch the brightest, happiest teapot she could find.

"Finally," said Clara as Maddie brought the pot to her table.

"It's not exactly what you ordered," said Maddie. "But I find on an upside-down kind of day, when your belly is full of thoughts and your head is full of butterflies, nothing quite puts things right like charm blossom tea. Watch…" She poured the avender-colored tea into Clara's cup. "When you talk, the tea…" The liquid began to stir on its own, rippling and spinning, pale lavender blending into peach and then orange. "It listens to your voice and becomes just the flavor you need."

Clara seemed too shocked to speak.

Maddie sat in the chair beside Clara, rested her chin on her hands, and smiled. "I started Ever After High last year, and I felt like the last teaspoon in the drawer. But then I met my best friend forever after, Raven Queen, and everything was as okay as pumpkin in pie. It will be for you, too. Especially since I put in extra honey."

Clara's posture slumped, just a little, and she looked into her cup of tea. "But my destiny isn't a very nice one, you know, even if I will be a queen. I become quite mean when I'm old, and what if the people at school don't like my fairytale, or my red hair, or me…?"

As she spoke, the tea turned a deep, deep purple. Clara lifted the cup and sipped. Her eyebrows rose.

The truth was, Maddie greatly enjoyed the upside-down kind of days. Especially because they always seemed to include a cup of warm tea with a great deal of honey.

The bell at the door rang, and a dark-haired girl with blue wings entered, clutching her hands, her eyes nervously taking in the scene.

"Over here!" Maddie waved. "Clara Lear has room at her table, and an entire pot of charm blossom tea."

"But…" Clara looked at Maddie, at the winged girl sitting down beside her, and again at Maddie. Suddenly her lips seemed to know what to do. They smiled. "We'll need scones, then, and a pot of fairyberry jam."

"Coming right up!" said Maddie.

Maddie skipped back to the kitchen, where her father thrust a cup in her hands.

"A new brew," he said, taking the scones and jam out to the table himself. "Fortune-teller tea. Give it a sip!"

The liquid was pink and smelled of strawberries, but when Maddie drank it, the flavor was deep and a little bitter, followed by a sudden burst of sweetness.

Her father returned. "Well?" he asked.

"It started out as black licorice and then melted into butterscotch," she said.

"Oh, my girl, the tea is telling you that this is the year to keep your ear to the ground and listen for surprises. Change is coming!"

Maddie's stomach was full of thoughts and her head full of butterflies. She checked her watch again. She couldn't wait for it all to begin.

From the Desk of
Madeline Hatter

The Mad Hatter of Wonderland's Haberdashery & Tea Shoppe

Teatime* Menu

* Teatime is any hour upon which a clock might point a hand at a number—unless the clock has no numbers, or no hands, which is an alarming thing, and a case of alarms can only be cured by sitting down immediately with a cup of tea and perhaps a cookie.

❧ TEA ❧

Tea served with lemon, honey, and a sugar swizzle stick

charm blossom
dragon scale
peppermint
chamomile
spritzle-fizzle
milkflower
chocolate rhubarb pumpkin raspberry dragon-fire
fortune-teller

*Note: Do not order Earl Grey unless you want
a dapper dormouse to appear in your teacup.*

❧ OTHER BEVERAGES ❧

Fizzy water is available in Berry Fine, Twisted Apple,
Cherry-Mint, and Cucumber-Watermelon flavors

❧ TREATS ❧

sugarplum biscuits served with fairyberry jam
scones served with fairyberry jam and cream
fairy finger sandwiches* (daily selection varies, Hatter's choice)
green tea fudge

Ask us about our tea party to-go packages!

*No cutlery provided. No fingers served.

Ashlynn Ella
(and the)
Mysterious Woodsman

ASHLYNN ELLA WOKE UP AT DAWN TO BIRDS singing at her window. But to Ashlynn's ears, it wasn't just tweeting; it was a conversation.

"*Good morning! The sun is up! Wake up! Time to eat,*" said the birds.

"Good morning," Ashlynn said back.

There was a clink of glass slippers against the wood floor, and then her mother appeared in the doorway. She had the same strawberry-blond hair and green eyes as Ashlynn. Her mother was already dressed, but Ashlynn didn't notice the clothes she was wearing. As always, her eyes went right to the glass slippers. Oh, how she loved those shoes.

"Chores, dear!" her mother said, leaning over to kiss the top of Ashlynn's head. "And then you should pack."

"Yes, Mother!"

Ashlynn washed her face, put on an apron, and then opened wide the door to her shoe closet. This princess wouldn't care if she wore a burlap sack every day, so long as she had dozens of footwear choices. Today she settled on a pair of strappy teal wedges and went to start breakfast. Even though her father's grand house came fully stocked with servants, her mother believed in good, solid, character-forming chores. After all, Ashlynn would inherit her mother's story and become the next Cinderella someday, and there would be lots of floors to mop and hearths to sweep before her Happily Ever After.

She bounded down the polished wood stairs and into the bustling kitchen, warmed by south-facing windows. The ecofriendly mansion was built from wood carefully harvested from the surrounding forest. The only things that excited her father, the king, more than a good ball were sustainable logging practices.

Ashlynn prepared a vegan porridge topped with wild blueberries and took a bowl upstairs.

"Breakfast, Auntie Step!" Ashlynn said, knocking before entering her aunt's room.

Auntie Step was brushing her hair at her vanity. She looked Ashlynn over and sniffed. "A proper porridge is made with milk."

"I suppose so," Ashlynn said, though she never cooked with animal products.

As usual, Auntie Step didn't say thank you, but Ashlynn didn't mind. The stepsister had had to be mean and nasty in Cinderella's story, and Ashlynn supposed that kind of meanness and nastiness didn't wear off, even after The End.

Still, having Auntie Step visit was good practice. After all, one day Ashlynn would have her own unkind stepsisters to put up with in the story, which would happen after her mother's untimely death, but Ashlynn didn't want to think about that part.

After cleaning up the dishes and watering the flowers, Ashlynn returned to her room. She was leaving tomorrow for boarding school at Ever After

High, and she hadn't even begun to pack. Perhaps, she admitted to herself, she had been hesitating just a little. While the other princesses at school shopped, chatted, and partied, Ashlynn worked at her after-school job at the Glass Slipper Shoe Store. And in her rare free moments, she usually fled to the nearest forest, just to feel like herself again.

This would be her second year at school, and so far she had yet to make a human friend who wanted to explore the outdoors with her. At least she had her pack of woodland pals.

Still, it was useless to waste another moment. She *must* pack. No sooner had she opened her closet and taken out a dress than a cottontail came hopping into her room.

"*Ashlynn!*" he said. "*My sisters are being so mean! And I can't find any clover blossoms! And, and...*" His fuzzy white nose trembled even harder, and he shook with a rabbit sob.

"Oh dear! I'll come help, of course," Ashlynn replied.

Those bunnies. Always so much drama! She supposed that was what happened when one lived in a hole with fifty brothers and sisters. Ashlynn looked at the dress in her hands. It was a hand-me-down coral silk from her mother, and she had been about to hem it so she could pack it.

Ashlynn leaned out her window and waved to a raccoon, who was sniffling around the rock garden hunting for snails. "Rocky, dear, could you be a darling and finish this for me?"

"*Certainly*," said Rocky, leaping onto her sill and into her room. He sat on a chair and threaded a needle. The raccoon had nimble fingers. Ashlynn gave him a quick kiss on his furry forehead and capered out the door after the bunny.

The woods were alive with voices.

"*Seeds! Seeds! Seeds!*"

"*I smell a worm. Mmm, juicy worm.*"

"*Scuttle, scuttle, scuttle....*"

Ashlynn smiled. So many friends.

But this morning, so many of her friends were in need. As soon as she finished helping with some sibling bonding at the rabbit warren, a trio of squirrels needed an arbitrator in the matter of whose cache of acorns was buried under a leaf. Then there was even more bunny drama, followed by a deer who couldn't find her favorite backscratching tree. Every time

Ashlynn was about to go home to pack, yet another animal emergency fell into her lap.

It was late afternoon when she followed cries for help to a fallen bird's nest. The mother robin was hopping around, shouting, "*My babies! My babies!*"

Three baby robins sat on the forest floor. They were uninjured from the fall, but they didn't yet have enough wing feathers to fly and would be easy prey there. Ashlynn sat down, placing the birds in her lap, and tried to mend the nest. It was a mess.

"Don't worry," she told the mother bird. "I'll work at it all night if I have to."

"*Boy in the woods*," a wren called from a tree.

"*A large boy walking under the oak tree*," a starling sang.

"*I smell a boy*," a hedgehog grumbled. "*He smells like pine.*"

Whoever this guy was, he didn't make a sound, but his every step was narrated by a chorus of wood-land creatures. Ashlynn didn't look, just listened.

"*Boy with a birdhouse.*"

"*A tall boy, hanging a birdhouse in a tree.*"

Hanging up a birdhouse? What unexpected kindness! If he wanted to be unseen, Ashlynn would pretend she didn't know he was there. It was darling, really, how stealthy he thought he was being. Actually, his steps *were* soundless. But when a girl can understand animal voices, it's hard to sneak up on her in the woods.

"*Birdhouse!*" said the mother bird, flapping away. "*It's perfect! It's perfect!*"

Ashlynn wanted desperately to peek. What did this boy with a birdhouse look like? Did she know him, perhaps? Certainly, it *couldn't* be one of those huntsmen who were always filling the woods with traps.

Ashlynn shivered.

She respected the kind of hero who was quiet and humble, who served for the pleasure of helping, not for the recognition. Her heart beat harder just at the thought of such a guy. And she couldn't help but turn around.

But the mysterious woodsman was gone.

Ashlynn sighed. That was for the best. Ashlynn was a princess, set to inherit a Happily Ever After. She was destined to marry some dashing, ball-planning prince, though she didn't yet know which one. It didn't really matter—all the princes she'd met seemed vaguely the same to her. They gelled their hair, whitened their teeth, and expected girls to swoon because of their smiles. And they most certainly didn't spend their free time roughing it in the deep woods making birdhouses.

She was absolutely forbidden from daydreaming about any nonprinces. No reason to even make the acquaintance of a friendly boy who builds houses for nest-less birds.

Ashlynn picked up the baby birds and placed them in the birdhouse, which had been cunningly made from branches, bark, and honeycomb. Whoever that boy was, he was incredibly skilled. Not to mention soft-hearted.

"*Good night!*" birds began to sing.

Good night? It was evening already, and she still hadn't mended her hand-me-downs or packed any clothes! Oh dear, she would be up all night now. Ashlynn picked up her mud-stained skirts and ran back home. She burst into her room.

Immediately her dress and apron sizzled into rags, a curse that struck anytime she was late—which was often. But she smiled anyway because her room was teeming with creatures.

There were the brother and sister bunnies, the doe with an itchy back, a stag with a pair of stockings stuck in his antlers, three raccoons with mending needles, several birds, and the trio of squirrels, still bickering over acorns while fitting shoes into her trunk.

Her closet was empty, her clothing trunk packed. The animals looked at her with shy, self-satisfied smiles.

"Thank you," Ashlynn said.

They gave her various pecks, nudges, and nuzzles before leaving.

Ashlynn's heart was still strangely pounding after the encounter in the woods. She shut her curtains, locked the door, and lifted her mattress, pulling out last year's Sustainable Logging Lumberjack Calendar. She flipped through the pages and sighed. Yes, the lumberjacks had chiseled jaws, warm eyes, and broad shoulders beneath flannel shirts. But it was the bios that made her heart go flutter-flap:

Mr. April enjoys roasting vegetables over a fire and the company of kind, modest young women.

*For every tree **Mr. May** takes down with a single ax stroke, he plants three seedlings with his own callused hands.*

*When **Mr. September** isn't hard at work lumberjacking, he loves to take his pet dogs on long walks.*

Ashlynn knew she shouldn't be looking at lumberjack calendars any more than she should be making friends with birdhouse-making guys. As the next Cinderella, she would have to marry whichever fairytale prince ended up in her story.

But she couldn't help making a small, secret wish that her assigned prince might be the kind who would grab her hand and run off into the woods— build a tree house with her or lie back and watch the stars come out through the canopy.

The kind of person who would make a birdhouse for a family of robins.

She didn't care about a fancy palace and loads of dresses. Just a cozy cottage somewhere—perhaps with an attached two-story, fully stocked shoe shed. And a guy with dirt under his fingernails and goodness in his heart.

From the Desk of
Ashlynn Ella

Sustainable Logging

Lumberjack Calendar

Get to Know Your Local Lumberjacks

 A virtuoso in the art of the feral hug, **Mr. January** is the only lumberjack to have hugged a mother bear and lived to tell the tale.

A gentleman and a scholar, **Mr. February** spends his free time searching for cures for willow rot and oak slough.

Mr. March works hard all day as a lumberjack, but after hours he plays hard...with his adorable pet kitten.

Mr. April enjoys roasting vegetables over a fire and the company of kind, modest young women.

For every tree **Mr. May** takes down with a single ax stroke, he plants three seedlings with his own callused hands.

Something of an architectural artisan, **Mr. June** designs plush new habitats for refugee rabbits.

Meat? No, thank you, says **Mr. July**, who in the evening hours manages a sustainable vegan café and karaoke bar called Turnip the Volume.

Mr. August sleeps on a cushion of soft moss under a pile of oak leaves, having long ago converted his personal cabin into an infirmary for sick and wounded animals.

When **Mr. September** isn't hard at work lumberjacking, he loves to take his pet dogs on long walks.

If **Mr. October** has one fault, it's caring too much.

Mr. November finds nothing so bracing in the morning as the smell of pinesap and omelets made with organic free-range eggs.

On winter evenings, **Mr. December** knits sweaters by the fire while humming show tunes....

Hunter Huntsman (and the) Forest Maiden

Tomorrow, Hunter Huntsman would be leaving for his second year of boarding school at Ever After High. Hunter Huntsman needed to pack.

He pulled out a drawer of his dresser and dumped the contents into a bag.

"There," he said heroically. "Packed."

That done, he grabbed his ax and went to breakfast. The cabin was small, so in good weather, his family dined outside.

"'Morning," said his mother as he came out of the

house. She was as tall as he was, her shoulders broad beneath her flannel shirt and denim overalls. A firm bun tamed her brown hair. "Packed?"

"Yea, ma'am," he said.

Hunter hung his ax beside his mother's on the ax stand.

"'Morning," said his father, hanging up his own ax. He looked a lot like his wife—just taller, broader, and full-bearded. "Packed?"

"Yes, sir," said Hunter.

"Pack?" said his baby sister, Fern, banging on her high chair with her tiny toy ax. "Pack, pack, pack!"

"You bet, Ferny," said Hunter, tickling her neck and speaking in a high voice. "You little teeny-cutesy baby, you!"

Fern giggled. Hunter's parents cleared their throats as if to say *No Huntsman should speak in a baby voice.* Hunter straightened and got to work eating.

He downed three huge bowls of porridge while trying to avert his gaze from the plate of sizzling bacon. Whenever he looked at it, all he could see was a cute little piggy face.

"Bacon?" said his mother.

"No, thanks."

The Castleteria at Ever After High had offered piles of veggies and fruit, soy turkey, and vegan sausage. He'd spent his first year there never eating anything that had once had a face. When he got home for the summer, he just couldn't go back to eating meat. Hunter hoped his parents hadn't noticed. A Huntsman a vegetarian? It was unthinkable!

"Since you're packed," said his father, "I could use your help out in the woods today."

"Of course!" said Hunter.

"I want to check my traps."

Hunter's huge and noble heart sank.

The three of them cleaned up the dishes and fetched their axes.

"Come back soon," said Hunter's mother, resting her ax on her shoulder. "I'll need you to watch Fern while I go chop down that lightning tree."

"Yes, ma'am," Hunter and his father said.

"Bye, Ferny!" Hunter said in a manly voice.

Fern banged her ax. "Bye-bye-bye!"

The woods were wet with dew and as sparkly in the morning sun as unicorn hair. Hunter followed his father, both holding their axes in Huntsman

Safety Pose—over one shoulder. They stepped on stones and tree roots to keep from leaving footprints. There was no danger, but a Huntsman never let his guard down.

Hunter's father was, after all, the very same Huntsman who'd refused to kill Snow White for the Evil Queen, the same Huntsman who'd come to Red Riding Hood's rescue. And one day Hunter would relive those same stories and play the same role as his father had. He had spent his whole life training for his hereditary fairytales.

They reached the first trap, sitting on the forest floor. Empty.

The Huntsman crouched by the wooden cage. "The spring mechanism was sprung, and I see squirrel hair in there, almost as if a squirrel was captured but opened the door and got away. Strange…"

"Yeah," said Hunter, loosening the neck of his faux-leather hooded shirt. "Strange."

They traveled to a trap hanging from a tree.

"Look at that," said the Huntsman. "Same thing. You'd almost think these animals are learning how to escape by themselves."

"Yeah, almost," said Hunter, wiping the sweat off his forehead.

The third trap was as large as a bear—and there were bear hairs inside but no bear.

"Huh," said the Huntsman, rubbing his chin. "I don't get it."

"Well, you know animals," said Hunter. "Wily as they come."

"I suppose…."

Hunter didn't like lying to his father. He shut his eyes and sighed.

"Tired, son?"

"Uh…no, I'm fine," said Hunter.

He *was* tired, in fact, but he didn't want to mention that he'd been up half the night just wandering the woods, finding his father's traps, breaking them open, and perhaps letting the cute, fuzzy animals inside run free. That information might not go down too well with his father.

Hunter first went on a solo hunt last summer. He'd tracked and cornered a fox, raised his ax, and heard mewing. Behind the fox, he had spied three baby foxes curled up, looking at him with large, dark, glistening eyes. He'd lowered his ax and never had the heart to hunt again.

Hunter was relieved to be returning to Ever After High. This summer had been exhausting, having sleepless nights and saving animals behind his father's back. A Huntsman who didn't want to hunt? Unthinkable!

They walked to the next trap, his father lecturing as they went.

"A Huntsman is loyal. A Huntsman is true. A Huntsman serves royalty unceasingly. A Huntsman heeds all cries for help—"

Just then, they heard a cry for help that sounded like this: "*Help!*"

Hunter and his father leaped into Huntsman Defense Stance—ax in one hand, the other hand held out, knees slightly bent, hair tossed by the breeze. They stood back-to-back, turning, listening to determine direction.

"Help!" came the call again.

"I'll save you!" the father and son cried in unison. Then, as had been Huntsman tradition for hundreds of years, they enacted the Huntsman-To-the-Rescue Move. With shoulders back, chests out, they tore off their shirts, showing that nothing—not even a shirt—could get between them and Saving the Day. The two Huntsmen held the pose while invisible trumpets played a heroic fanfare.

Hunter was never sure where those trumpets were or what magic made them play. But he liked them.

Father and son ran south through the woods at the speed of rampaging bulls.

"Help!" a man in farmer garb was crying on the ground, holding his ankle.

"We're here!" said the Huntsman. "What is the trouble?"

"I was looking for firewood, and I saw...I saw...I swear I saw...a wolf!" said the man. "And I started to run, but I fell and twisted my ankle, and any second that wolf might come back and eat me!"

A wolf? In these woods? No wolf would dare roam so close to his father's home, Hunter thought. But they had to be sure. Leave a wolf to itself, and next thing you know it's breaking into a grandma's house and shedding all over her nightgowns.

"I'll go scout," said Hunter.

His father nodded. He picked up the man in

both arms and began to carry him back to the man's house.

Hunter got on his knees and searched for wolf tracks. He recognized the prints of deer, a moose, a badger, several squirrels, a family of bunnies, and a fox with a sliver in its paw (poor fox)—but no wolf. The man had probably just seen the badger and gotten nervous. But just to be certain, Hunter ranged out farther.

He spent all day in his search; all Huntsmen had a creed: No matter how often someone cries wolf, always take it seriously. It was almost evening, and he was about to return home when he heard the desperate tweeting of a robin in trouble.

Hunter didn't need to do the Huntsman-To-the-Rescue Move again. That was just for people saving. A good thing, too, because he didn't have a second shirt.

In Huntsman Stealth Mode, he ran through the brush and around trees in absolute silence. Up ahead, he could see a mother robin on the forest floor hopping around her fallen nest. But before he could get any closer—there was a girl. A girl with strawberry-blond hair and a simple working dress, the kind a maidservant might wear. She crouched down and tried to mend the nest.

He couldn't be sure from the back, but he thought she looked familiar. Could she be a fellow student at Ever After High? Her kindness melted his heart like a chunk of butter in porridge. And the plaintive tweets from the mother bird were enough to bring a tear to his eye.

Hunter fetched some tree bark, pine boughs, and a honeycomb. A few minutes later, he had made a handsome birdhouse. More of a bird castle, really. He could make almost anything from whatever tools he had on hand. His father used that innate Huntsman skill to make traps and weapons. What would he think if he knew his son had used it to make a birdhouse? Or even a bird castle?

Using Huntsman Stealth Steps, Hunter crept up to a tree behind the girl's back, hung the bird castle on a high branch, and retreated.

From the branches of a far-off tree, Hunter watched the girl discover the bird castle. He couldn't make out her face from that distance, but her gestures of happiness made his heart glow. And the delighted chirping of the birds put a gooey smile on his face.

His heart beat harder. Maybe he should go introduce himself. Maybe he and this forest maiden could become friends and, like, go on a date or something—but, no. Hunter stopped himself. This year at school was his Legacy Year. In a few short weeks, he would sign the Storybook of Legends and promise to become his generation's Huntsman in the tales of Snow White and Little Red Riding Hood. Meeting—dating?—a kind forest maiden was not part of his destiny.

Besides, a breeze reminded him that his shirt was torn. The Huntsman-To-the-Rescue Move had unfortunate consequences.

So Hunter put his ax over his shoulder, turned his back to the girl, and hurried home. But on the way he did something he'd never done before—he allowed himself to daydream.

Dexter Charming

(and the)

Yellow-Eyed Changeling

"FAMILY BALL!" SHOUTED DARING CHARMING, barreling into his brother Dexter's room without a knock. Dexter had just enough time to take off his glasses and set them on his desktop before his just-barely-older brother tackled him.

Daring made "Family Ball" sound like some kind of wrestling game. But really, it was just the weekly get-together at their grandparents' castle with all of Dexter's uncles, aunts, and cousins, where they would eat, talk, and just be…Charming. Only a ballroom was large enough to hold the whole clan, so it was a Family Ball, rather than a barbecue or picnic or shindig.

Daring loved the event so fiercely that he only seemed able to express his excitement by wrestling Dexter to the ground. After years of grappling with taller, heavier, and stronger Daring, Dexter had learned a few moves. He could usually twist just right to keep from getting pinned immediately. Sometimes he even got enough leverage to flip Daring and break free. For a moment, anyway. But his brother always kept coming. Even though it was just play, Daring Charming never stopped fighting until he won.

"Family Ball!" Daring shouted again, pinning one of Dexter's arms to the floor with his knee.

Dexter locked his legs around Daring's foot and pulled, but his brother was too strong to move.

"Ha-ha!" Daring bellowed. "Nice try, little brother!"

Dexter kicked, only managing to pull the back of his brother's shoe off, but that had been his plan. He darted his eyes to the left and put on his best worried expression.

"No!" he shouted. "She's going to fall!"

Daring leaped up to catch whatever girl, woman, or female animal was in danger and stumbled on the heel of his half-off shoe.

Dexter took the opening and sprang onto his brother's back.

"Ha-ha!" he shouted, locking his arm around Daring's neck.

Daring made a small *urk* noise and then fell flat on his back. Which is to say, on top of Dexter. The air rushed out of the younger Charming's lungs. As Dexter struggled to suck back in all that air, Daring took to his feet, planted one (now bare) foot on Dexter's chest, and mimed a sword stroke to his brother's neck.

"Yield, little brother!" Daring proclaimed. "Lest you miss the festivities of the Family Ball!"

Dexter let out a hoarse laugh. "I yield," he rasped.

"Then I shall spare you." Daring smiled his brilliant, white-toothed smile. He helped Dexter to his feet. "Good misdirection on the falling-girl bit. I should have remembered you wouldn't be able to see anything without your glasses on."

"'A hero uses whatever is at hand,'" Dexter said, quoting one of their father's favorite pieces of advice.

"Right you are, my four-eyed bro," Daring said. "Anyway, Mom wants us on the tram to Grandpa's castle in five minutes. Let Darling know. I'll go ahead and secure the path, make sure there aren't any dragons or ogres lurking about."

"Sure thing," Dexter said. There was no path to the tram, other than the driveway in front of their castle, and any dragons or ogres that might show up were more likely to be offering bouquets of flowers to their sister than to be attacking. But it made Daring happy to "secure" things, so Dexter let it go.

Dexter heard Daring shout "Family Ball!" one more time as his footsteps receded down the hallway.

Dexter plopped back down in front of his desk and put on his glasses.

"Family Ball," he mumbled.

From his own mouth, it didn't sound like a tackling game so much as a tedious beauty pageant in which he always came in last place.

A message popped up on his desktop mirror.

REMINDER: Pack! Legacy Year starts
tomorrow! --CharDex

He'd set the reminder months ago. As if he was going to forget. Legacy Year was the year he would finally learn his destiny. Everyone took as fact that Daring would be getting the Prince Charming role from the Snow White story. That was the highest-profile destiny open to a Charming this year and Daring was certainly the highest-profile Charming around. Unlike most children of fairytale parents, Charmings didn't always inherit their parents' exact story. That would be weird. In that case, Apple White would be the next Snow White like her mother, but her prince would have to be her father's son, requiring her to marry her brother. Handily, there were loads of Charmings to take up those spare destinies.

Dexter chewed a nail down to his fingertip. He really had *no idea* what destiny the Storybook of Legends would show him when he signed. It was roughly time for a new Beast, and he'd overheard his parents whispering that they hoped his destiny would align him as the next Beauty's prince. But that would mean he was destined to marry Rosabella Beauty, and no chance that…that Raven Queen… never mind. He scolded himself for even hoping.

With his luck, he'd get some obscure tale that required him to run back and forth through a glass tunnel in his underwear until he died. Or worse…was the Marsh King up for a new heir? Dexter shuddered.

Just a few more weeks and he'd know. Even if his destiny was horrible or embarrassing or Raven-less, at least he'd *know*.

He was looking in the mirror, trying to comb down stubborn hair that stuck straight up no matter what he did, when a message from Daring popped open.

REMINDER: FAMILY BAAAALLLLLLL!!!
~IMCharming

Dexter laughed. His smile was nothing like Daring's—not as blinding, not as bold, a little shy and unsure. He pulled back his shoulders and lifted his chin, checking out his reflection in the mirror. His smile melted. He straightened his glasses, his shoulders slumping.

"I'm ready," his sister, Darling, called from his door. "You know, in case you were supposed to get me to take me to the tram before Mom got mad."

"Oh!" Dexter said, standing so quickly he bumped his knee on the bottom of the desk. "Ow."

"You okay?" Though Darling and Dexter were siblings, his hair was all dark brown and stubborn forelock, while hers was all pale blond locks and easy elegance. Even now, she looked dressed for the fairest of fairytale balls—the dancing kind, not the family-dinner-games-wrestling-storytelling kind. Dexter wasn't well-versed in girls or clothing, but it seemed to him that their mother kept Darling in especially fancy stuff.

"Yes, er, fine," Dexter said, limping to the door. "I just lost track of time."

An incredibly loud and slightly angry female shout sounded from outside Dexter's window. "WE ARE LEAVING!"

"We'd better run!" Dexter said.

"Wait, just close your eyes for a second," Darling said. She stuck her head out the window. "Hey, guys!"

Dexter watched as Darling waved at the rest of the family waiting by the tram in the courtyard below. As soon as they were all looking at her, she tossed her hair.

Oh no, Dexter thought as everything around him slowed to a crawl. Darling became a blur as she darted toward him.

"Itoldyoutocloseyoureyes," she said, almost too fast for him to follow.

He should have known better. She'd done this before when pressed for time. Just tossed her hair and made the world go slow-mo.

"Ughyou'resoslow," Darling said super-fast, tugging at his hand.

"Soooorrrrryyyy," Dexter slurred.

"FineI'mjustgoingtocarryyou," Darling said, and heaved Dexter up onto her shoulder. The hallways blurred around him. He didn't even have time to say "Wait! This is such an unprincely position! And wow! I knew you were strong, but you can actually carry me? Wow!" before Darling set him down just outside the courtyard.

Darling put a finger to her lips as time started to speed up again. "Don't tell anyone I did that," she said, and ran out to the tramway.

The courtyard overlooked the valley below, which was inscribed with pretty blue rivers winding through green farms. The family castle was perched on a mountaintop, unscalable cliffs all around. Atop each mountain in the same range, the other Charming castles balanced, the line of homes connected by aerial tramways. The tram was like a ferryboat in the sky, powered by ogres, giants, or Very Large Men pulling ropes at either end. Dexter supposed it was a cool thing, but he always got a little anxious seeing all that space between him and the ground.

"Face the fear and it will disappear!" his dad always said, so every time they rode the tram to a relative's castle, Dexter stood close to the windows and looked down. It was still scary.

He joined his family inside the tiny space, and the tram car sprang into motion. They slowly crossed over the stomach-dropping depths of the valley to the mountaintop courtyard of Palace Charming East, where Grandpa Auspicious and Grandma Alluring lived.

The tram jerked to a stop and the doors swung open.

"Welcoming to Palace Charming East," bellowed the tram ogre from outside. "Are you needing out-coming assistance?"

"We're fine, my good fellow, just fine," Dexter's

father said, spinning as he leaped from the tram, landing with his hand in perfect position for his mother to grab as she daintily stepped out. Daring followed, enacting almost the same move as his father, his hand out for Darling. She grabbed it, and then swung down on his arm like it was a piece of playground equipment. Daring laughed, but their mother's cluck of disapproval was audible to everyone.

"Would you like a hand, brother?" Daring said, winking.

"No, thanks, Prince Monkeybars." Dexter hopped to the ground with almost as much flair as Daring, but he turned his ankle a bit. He hoped no one noticed his wince.

"Daring!" a tiny shout issued from the castle, and a little red tornado closed the distance between them, pouncing on Daring with a growl.

"I am attacked," bellowed Daring, "by the Dread Prince Courageous! Unhand me, beast!"

The little boy scampered atop, around, and behind Daring. "And you are Dragon-Devil Daring, here to be slain!" He put Daring in a headlock and squeezed.

"Aggggh!" Daring howled dramatically, falling to his knees. "I am slain! Agh!"

The boy hopped off, smiling proudly. He nodded to Dexter. "Good to see you, Dexter."

"Uh, you too, Dread Prince—" Dexter began, but the boy was already engaging Daring in enthusiastic talk about his tower-climbing lessons. Several more young cousins ran screaming at Daring, dog-piling him with squeals of laughter.

Dexter watched. He put his hands in his pockets. He took them out again.

Darling grabbed Dexter's hand. "All right, brother," she whispered to him, face determined. "We can do this."

Together, brother and sister entered Palace Charming East. The ballroom was high, wide, and chock-full of aunts, uncles, cousins. All perfectly Charming. Dexter froze, determined not to run away but feeling, as always, not quite Charming enough.

"Darling!" called out a group of tiara-wearing girls. They approached as a single unit, like some pastel-colored beast with a dozen princess heads. There was his youngest aunt, Fairest; his cousins Beauteous, Breathtaking, and Beloved, and

Courageous's sisters Cherished and…was that Charity? She looked different to him somehow.

He felt Darling stiffen next to him and then let go of his hand. She took a breath and then slowly made her way toward the other princesses. She looked back at him. She looked sort of sad—uncomfortable for sure. Some Charmings were more charming than others, he supposed, leaning back against the wall beside a painting of a flower.

A wallflower, he thought, smirking at himself. *How appropriate.*

Eventually they would start playing family games, like Stab the Tail on the Dragon, Catch the Princess, Duck Duck Cockatrice, and Bag. Dexter didn't mind playing Bag, which was really just like Tag except when you got tagged, the person who was "it" put you in a bag and dragged you around with them. Dexter had spent a lot of his younger years in a bag. The smell of burlap still made him feel motion-sick.

"Leg of goat?" a gruff voice sounded beside him. To his credit, Dexter didn't scream out from surprise, but he was definitely startled by the abrupt appearance of a half-ogre servant holding a platter of meat.

"Er...no, thank you," Dexter stammered, adding "would *you* like one?" and then almost kicking himself. It wasn't *Charming* to offer a servant what they'd just offered you.

The half ogre's eyes widened. "Don't mind if I do." He picked up a goat leg and took a bite. "Gordon," he said.

"Gore dawn?" Dexter asked.

"Gordon. It's my name," Gordon said. "Typically now you tell me your name and say 'pleased to meet you' or 'I really must be going now.'"

"Oh, I'm Dexter. Dexter Charming."

Gordon nodded, disengaging his hand. "I guessed the Charming part."

Dexter winced. He couldn't even out-charm an ogre servant.

Gordon pointed at the painting with the goat leg. "Wallflower. Heh."

"Yeah..."

Gordon squinted his eyes, scrutinizing Dexter. "I wonder if we have something in common, Dexter Charming. See, I'm half ogre. Not ogrish enough for my ma, not man enough for my da. Awkward business, always feeling like I never measure up."

"How do you do it?" Dexter asked. "I mean, you seem, er...well adjusted enough...."

"For an ogre?" Gordon laughed. He ripped the remaining meat off the goat leg with blunt teeth and stuffed the bone in his pocket. "After a while, you figure out who you want to be, then you be that."

Easy for an ogre to say—even a half ogre. Dexter couldn't choose who he would be. The Storybook of Legends would do that for him.

Gordon took out a handkerchief and wiped his mouth. "I should get back to my duties. Thanks for the leg, and try to remember you've got something none of them have."

Gordon walked away.

Dexter adjusted his glasses. The only thing he had that no other Charming did was poor vision. How many times at Family Ball had some game gotten rough and some cousin had "accidentally" broken his glasses? Of course, sometimes losing his ability to see made him appreciate when he could. Encouraged him to look more closely, perhaps.

His eyes scanned the crowd. Daring was having a ball, as one should at a Family Ball, tossing the smaller Charmings back and forth with cousin

Earnest. Dexter was just thinking what an excellent King Charming his brother would make when Daring got distracted by a wall mirror. He was so busy checking himself out that he nearly missed catching one of the little cousins.

Well, no one is perfect.

Darling was as beautiful as ever, smiling, captivating the other princesses with some story. Probably to everyone she looked Charmingly perfect, but Dexter noticed a small wrinkle between her eyes. Something about these gatherings exhausted her.

His cousin Charity started to turn his way. He smiled at her, and she looked back with eyes that weren't hers.

Dexter blinked. She was smiling at Darling now and laughing at the story, seeming totally normal. But for a fraction of a second, he'd swear her eyes had been *yellow*. A trick of the light?

"Girls! Girls!" Grandma Alluring called out. "I would like all young ladies to attend me, please!"

As the princesses followed Grandma out, Dexter's eyes caught again on Charity. She seemed perfectly Charming, walking daintily in her crystalline shoes. Dexter narrowed his eyes. There was dirt on the bottoms of Charity's shoes! Mud, maybe. Charming princesses never had dirty shoes.

"Boys! Boys!" his grandfather called. "Would all the young men please attend me?"

Dexter was swept up in a crowd of Charmings marching toward their eldest relative. Dexter craned his head back to keep spying on Charity.

"Today," Dexter's grandfather was saying, "in honor of many of you starting a new school year, but mostly because I was bored…" He paused, waiting for the laughter of his audience to fade. "Today, I am sending you…"

Grandpa looked around as if to make sure his wife had left the room. Then he leaped atop the mile-long dining table and held his fists in the air. "…on a quest!"

All the male Charmings cheered. Dexter did, too, a little later than the rest. Dexter supposed a nice friendly trivia contest or karaoke party had been too much to hope for.

Grandpa Auspicious was still tall and broad, with a tremendous white beard that wiggled when he laughed. As a young man, he had been known as Siegfried, hero of a series of tales, outlandish adventures, and mythological triumphs. But he married a Charming princess, and so while one of his sons had inherited the Siegfried story, the rest became Charming princes.

Honestly, the Charming family tree was so complicated one of the daughters of the Three Fates dedicated her entire life to tracking and recording it.

"I have hidden various treasures from my heroic escapades around the palace." Grandfather cocked an eyebrow, and his voice went low and mysterious. "Some may be guarded...."

A chorus of "Huzzah!" and "Not for long!" sounded from the audience.

"All will require the talents of a true Charming to find and retrieve them."

Most of the princesses had followed Grandma into the drawing room, but Charity lagged behind. She paused at a serving table and examined a knife. She wasn't going to take it, was she? The crowd of boys jostled, obscuring Dexter's view, and by the time he could spot Charity again, she was closing the drawing room door after her.

If he had seen truly and she had yellow eyes, what would that mean? A magical curse, perhaps?

He scolded himself for even worrying about it. After all, he was in a room full of Prince and King Charmings. Their destinies were to save, rescue, root evil and danger out of every dragon lair and rabbit hole. There was no way that Dexter, the least heroic of all of them, could notice a danger first.

"…the Spiked Globe of Grub-Sal can be found by he with the heart of an eagle," his grandfather was saying.

Prince Charmings had begun to sneak off from the group to get a head start on the treasure seeking. Dexter had missed descriptions of the first few, but if he was competing with the likes of Daring and Earnest, surely Dexter wouldn't find any of them anyway.

"…the pinned mask of Lord Cenobitious to the strong, the Soaring Sword of Salamander Steve to those of capacious lung, the Gauntlets of Elven Food to the brash, and lastly, the Crochet Hook of Aunt Arachne to the truly fearless. Go now, my progeny! Go and conquer!"

Everyone remaining took off in a run, Dexter included. He raced beside his cousin Fearless for a while, and then turned off into a side hall that looked completely Charming-free. Slowing to a walk, he went through the motions of searching for treasure—lifting up tapestries, knocking on bookcases, opening drawers.

Dexter looked under a table, upended an empty vase, and then sat down on a divan. A heroic cry of "Aha!" echoed from down the hallway.

Dexter stared at the tiled floor. He supposed he could just sit here until everything was wrapped up, but that was boring, and there was dirt on the floor. He blinked. His own observation had caught him off guard. But he was right. There was dirt on the floor. Just a little, but enough to be noticeable if you happened to be staring at it. Which he was.

Dexter crouched close to the dirt. It was a footprint. And there was another in front of it. And another. Usually, Grandma Alluring's castle was spotless.

Yellow-eyed Charity had had dirt on her shoes.

He followed the dirt scuffs all the way up to a hallway closet and opened it without hesitation, like any Charming would. Unfortunately, in this case, that bold choice didn't serve him so well.

Icy hands grabbed Dexter by the neck, yanking him inside the closet, the door closing behind him with a quiet click. He struggled to breathe. Yellow eyes, unnaturally bright in the darkness of the closet, stared into his.

"How do you know?" asked a sweet female voice.

Dexter tried to squeak out the words "Please let me go," but managed only a pathetic wheeze. He clawed at the fingers around his neck, but they were cold and hard, like a stone statue.

"You cannot know. No one can know. Those are the rules."

"Ch-Charity?" Dexter managed to rasp.

The grip loosened, just a bit.

"Yes," the sweet voice hissed. "Charity. That is who I am."

"No...it isn't. What did you do with Charity?"

The grip tightened, and not-Charity threw him to the ground.

"*I am Charity now!*" it screeched.

Distant footsteps sounded.

"I hear a fiend!" someone yelled from beyond the closet door.

Dexter ran his fingers back and forth across the floor. Many of the closets in this castle had a trapdoor or a laundry chute.

"Is this what you're looking for?" not-Charity said. She pulled a lever mounted in the rear wall, and a square of floor swung open. Unfortunately, Dexter, not the not-Charity, was over it.

His stomach seemed to yank free of his middle as he fell through a winding stone shaft, bumping his elbows and scraping his knees until finally coming to a hard thump on a stone floor covered in straw. From above him he heard the distant echoes of not-Charity cry in a falsely sweet voice, "Help! Oh, won't some brave prince help me, please!"

Then the sound of the trapdoor clicking shut.

Dexter coughed, groaned, and patted himself down for broken bones. He was in a dark, dank cage, the stone floor dirty with rotting straw. The dungeon. If Daring found out, he'd tease him till Little Bo Peep's sheep came home.

"Is that you, Dexter?" a voice called from beyond the bars.

A non-yellow-eyed Charity was lounging on a wooden bench in an adjacent cell, reading an ornate red book by the light of a candle.

"Charity?" Dexter rasped.

"Yeah," she said.

"Are you okay?"

"Me? Oh, totally. Just reading."

Dexter stood to go to her, but there was no door to his cell. "Aren't you trapped?"

Charity looked around her. "In here? No."

"It looks like you're trapped."

"Well, I can't *actually* get out, if that's what you mean. But I don't want to at the moment. Can you come save me in, like, a couple of hours?"

"I'm trapped, too," Dexter said.

"Can't you break through the bars or anything?"

"I don't think so." He looked around, just to double check. "I mean, there isn't even a door."

"I guess you'll have to wait for a Prince Charming to save you, too, then," Charity said, her gaze drifting back to her book. "I have spare books you could read, but I only have the one candle."

"You know there's something going on up there, right?"

"Yes. The Family Ball." She rolled her eyes.

"No, I mean, um, there's a…a…creature that looks like you."

"The changeling. Sure." She put down her book

as if slightly annoyed that he was still talking and began to dig through a knapsack.

"A *changeling*?" Dexter asked. "Like, a real changeling? Here?"

"Here, I have some crochet stuff," Charity said, tossing a ball of red yarn stuck with a crochet hook through the bars. "You want that? Something to keep you occupied while I read?"

"The changeling is pretending to be you," Dexter said, his voice cracking a little. "And it is super-creepy."

Charity sighed. "I *know*. I bought the wooden changeling doll off the Mirror Network, brought it here, and did the spell so it could be me for a little while. If I just hid away somewhere to read, the family would scour the woods, overturn tables, shout curses, and slay monsters to get me back. And when they found me, I'd have to go to the Ball anyway."

"So you...got a changeling, a notoriously unstable and vengeful magical creature, and gave it permission to look like you."

Charity shrugged. "It seemed like a good idea

at the time. When it locked me in here and did that screechy laugh, I did start to wonder...."

"But...but...aren't you worried? You aren't screaming, or upset, or anything!"

"Oh, I'll do that if no one finds me by the time I finish my book."

She tucked back into it, her eyes scanning the pages hungrily, and he knew she'd already forgotten about him.

Dexter looked around the cell. His dad always said, "For a Charming, there is always a way out." He ran his hands against the walls. Slimy, but no secret doors. He crawled around the floor. Dirty, but no keys, tools, or useful carved messages. He jumped, scrabbling at the edge of the ceiling hole he'd fallen through, but there was no ledge to grab.

He picked up the ball of yarn from the dirty cell floor and dislodged the crochet hook. Would it be worse for his cousins to find him in a cell doing nothing, or to find him in a cell with a half-finished cozy winter hat on his lap?

"Do you know how to crochet?" Charity called from her cell. "Maybe you can crochet a rope or something to escape."

The crochet hook was silver, about the size of a dinner fork, with black lettering along the shaft: PROPERTY OF ARACHNE.

"Hey!" Dexter called. "Where did you find this?"

Charity didn't even glance up from her book. "In the sewing salon, duh. Grandma has tons of craft stuff: lace, looms, scrapbooking materials. You know, the pink room on the third floor? Smells like roses?"

Dexter had never ventured inside the pink room. It had always seemed to be just for girls. What had Grandpa said? "The Crochet Hook of Aunt Arachne to the truly fearless." Dexter chuckled to himself. Grandpa had been gambling that the princes would be afraid to go into Grandma's room. Undaunted by dragons and ogres but scared of a rose-smelling pink room? He chuckled again.

"What does the crochet hook do?" he asked Charity.

She looked up from her book with an expression he imagined she reserved only for people who suddenly revealed themselves to be utterly, surprisingly stupid. "It crochets," she said. "It is a *crochet hook*."

"Oh," Dexter muttered, cheeks coloring. He was glad it was dark in the dungeon.

"Though technically I suppose it un-crochets, too," Charity said, turning back to her book. "That one has a tiny wire thingie at the end that pulls yarn out, good for unpicking a mistake. No Charming princess ever needs that end, of course."

Dexter grunted. He was sure that if he ever took up crocheting, he would definitely have to use the unpicking thingy. All he made were mistakes. Upstairs his cousins and brothers were probably congratulating themselves on all the puzzles they'd solved, treasures they'd uncovered, monsters they'd defeated, while he was trapped in a dungeon.

"Ugh!" Dexter threw the crochet hook.

Thunk.

Dexter had been expecting a *clink*. Or the way his luck usually went, the *snap* of the hook breaking.

"Are you finally doing something heroic over there?" Charity asked.

The crochet hook had wedged itself into solid stone like a dart into corkboard. Dexter gave it a little tug, and it stayed put. He put up his foot and pulled harder, finally dislodging it. The silver was unscratched and glinted like a dragon's eye in the candlelight.

Dexter jumped up, jabbing the hook into the stone just inside the opening in the ceiling. It held, but he didn't. The sweat on his palms betrayed him, and he lost his grip, falling to the floor.

"Okay," Dexter said, wiping his palms on his trousers. "I can do this. I *am* a Charming."

"Did you say something?" Charity asked.

"Er, yes!" Dexter said. He put his fists on his hips heroically, even though Charity's gaze was locked on her page. "I will return quickly to save you from your prison!"

"Don't rush if the Family Ball is still on," said Charity.

Dexter jumped and grabbed the crochet hook again. This time he didn't slip, but it took several awkward twists, pulls, and swings to leverage himself back up into the tunnel. The cramped space allowed him to brace himself, feet pushing against one side, back against the other. Slowly he ascended, pulling out the hook, sticking it in a few feet higher, and then wriggling up to it. It was a lot like the rock climbing he did with his brother in the summer, except there was no sun, no rope, and no one to catch him if he fell.

After an exhausting adventure of dirt smears, knee bumps, and elbow scrapes, Dexter reached the iron plate of the trapdoor. No amount of pushing or pulling made it budge. He felt along the walls for a catch, a button, or a lever, something that might open the door, but found nothing but the rusty hinges of the door itself. One time Daring had removed the bolts in the hinges of Dexter's bedroom door so that it fell off when Dexter tried to use it. Maybe that would work here.

He tapped at the bolt holding the two halves of the hinge together with the crochet hook. Nothing. He tapped a little harder, and the metallic clang was too loud for his comfort. The not-Charity thing might still be lurking above.

His legs burned and trembled from trying to hold himself in the vertical tunnel. He glanced at the long drop and gulped, closed his eyes, and concentrated. Maybe the hinges were rusted. Maybe they just needed to be scraped clean, and then he could push the bolts free. Flipping the needle around to use the wire hook that was the "un-crocheting" end, Dexter scraped at the head of the fastening bolt. With the first touch of the wire to metal, the hinge collapsed. The two halves of the hinge and the bolt holding them together dropped into the abyss below.

Dexter stared, openmouthed, at the hook for a few seconds. Then he shrugged, and scraped the other hinge. The exact same thing happened, the two hinge halves and bolt falling away. Now there was nothing to hold the trapdoor in place. It thumped painfully on Dexter's head, slipped past him, and clattered all the way down the tunnel, making more noise than a goblin blacksmith.

Dexter scrambled up out of the hole and collapsed on the closet floor. His head hurt. His everything hurt. But he needed to move. He had just enough time to crawl to his knees when the closet door swung open and quickly closed again.

"You!" The yellow-eyed Charity hissed. "I am not normally a stabby sort of changeling, but I can make an exception for you!"

The creature pulled the dinner knife from the folds of its dress and charged.

Dexter was tired and weak and in an enclosed space, but he was still a Prince Charming. He dodged the first blow. The changeling swung again and Dexter spun, catching the knife arm. He moved to twist the arm behind the creature, but it was strong. Surprisingly strong. The changeling shoved hard and sent him sprawling against the closet wall, scattering various cleaning supplies.

"A hero uses whatever is at hand," he muttered, grabbing a mop and swinging it like a club.

The wood shattered on the creature's head, and it hissed, yanking the remains of the mop from Dexter's hands. Dexter rolled, grabbing a bucket. The changeling took another stab, and Dexter thrust the bucket at the blade. The knife embedded itself in the wood of the bucket, and Dexter twisted it sharply. There was a crack, and the blade of the knife snapped from its handle.

The creature screeched, throwing the handle to the floor. "I do not need a knife! My hands are enough!"

Dexter tried to shield himself with the bucket, but the changeling tore it away, and those cold, hard hands gripped his neck again. Dexter kicked it in the shins, but that was like kicking a stone wall.

"You will die," it said. "But I will tell them you saved me from a monster first. So they won't know you for the weakling you are. Be glad in your death!"

There was a glint on the floor.

Dexter went down on his knees as if overwhelmed, but really he just needed to…reach…the…crochet… hook. He got his fingers around it and held it up like a sword.

The creature began to laugh a hoarse, screechy, mocking laugh.

But Dexter flipped the crochet hook to the un-doing end and swiped.

With a sound like a wet thunderclap, the laughter stopped, the creature vanished, and Dexter fell on his face.

The closet door swung open. "Defend yourself, beast!" Daring shouted. Dexter groaned and rolled onto his back.

"What? Dexter?" Daring climbed into the closet. "Was that *you* making all those high-pitched screech-monster sounds?"

"Um," Dexter noised, struggling to his feet. A wooden doll lay on the closet floor, a troll-faced sculpture about six inches long with a very angry expression on its face. The changeling unmade.

"You're filthy, brother!" Daring said. "Have you been chimney-sweeping this whole time?"

Dexter gave the troll-faced doll a kick, sending it tumbling down the open trapdoor.

"Come on," Daring said, leading Dexter into the hallway. "You can help me treasure hunt. The only one left is—" Daring grabbed Dexter's hand, examining the crochet hook. "By the unseemly foot of the basilisk, you've got it!"

Daring pulled Dexter into the ballroom. Most of the family had returned from the hunt, many showing off capes and swords and booties and orbs.

"Behold the fearless champion!" Daring bellowed.

Everyone cheered.

Darling rushed over to Dexter. "What happened to you?"

He grimaced, realizing he must be filthy, bruised, and scraped up.

"Charity. And there was a changel—"

He broke off when some cousins and uncles lifted him up in the air, carrying him on their shoulders.

"In the dungeon!" Dexter called back to Darling.

Darling nodded and darted away just as all the Prince Charmings broke into song.

For he's a jolly good Charming!
For he's a jolly good Charming!
Let's give him a piece of pie!

Several forkfuls of charmberry-rhubarb pie later, Darling joined him at the incredibly long banquet table.

"Charity's back with her family," Darling whispered. "No one noticed she was missing."

"How did you even get her out?"

"I picked the dungeon door lock and then forced the bars of her cell with a steel spear," Darling said. "Don't tell anyone. Mother...wouldn't approve."

"You forced the..." Dexter stared at his sister.

Darling darted her eyes around. "Stop staring at me. Try to act normal."

"That's just awesome," Dexter said. "That's all. I mean, I always knew you were awesome, just not in so many different ways."

"Let's keep those extra ways between us, okay? Charity said she's going to pretend nothing happened, and I'm good with that."

"All right," Dexter said. "I just...you know, I

defeated a changeling, which was my first real monster, and nobody knows."

"*I* know," Darling said.

"That's true," Dexter said.

"And you did retrieve the Crochet Hook of Aunt Arachne. Everyone knows that."

"But Charity was the fearless one really," Dexter said. "I guess I just wish … I wish …"

He hesitated to say more. There were lots of things he wished, but wishes were often magic, and Prince Charming destinies were not ones of magic but of heroism. But if he'd been a wood-carver looking up at a star, or an orphaned Cinderella visiting her mother's grave, he'd have wished to know his destiny and somehow feel prepared to face it.

Darling grabbed his hand and raised it over his head. "All hail the fearless champion of the crochet hook!" she shouted.

A chorus of "Huzzah!" and "Hear! Hear!" sounded around the room.

Dexter smiled and shrugged. "All hail me," he said.

Darling Charming
(and the)
Razor Eel

DARLING CHARMING KNEW IT WAS A MISTAKE to walk out onto her balcony. But when she opened the window, clean, cool mountain air rushed in, beckoning her like a crooked finger into the morning.

She thought, *Maybe it's still early enough. Maybe no one is up. Maybe no one will see me....*

So she stepped out.

Her room was in a grand turret of Charming Castle, built atop the craggy peak of a mountain. She felt like an eagle in its aerie, the sky as close as the swipe of her fingers, the whole world laid out at her feet—patchwork farms in green valleys; villages and towns clustered along the bends in rivers; a chain of mountains, each topped with a castle for the many branches of the huge Charming family. She stretched out her arms. The wind batted her long white nightgown and long white-blond hair, and for a moment, she almost believed she could fly.

A loud knock on the massive front doors reverberated throughout the castle. She heard the butler call her from downstairs.

"Princess Darling! There are two farmer boys and an ogre at the door who want to know if you'll marry one of them! Oh, and here comes something scaly that might be a dragon! He says he would like to propose as well!"

"Dragon?" she heard her big brother Daring shout. "Ogre? You are warned! How dare you so much as look upon my sister! Today you meet your *doom*!"

There were sounds of fighting, some roars, the hiss of spit fire. She caught a glimpse of the group spilling down the front steps and out into the courtyard.

Darling sighed. She stepped back inside her room and shut her balcony door. How had the farmers even seen her from the village below? Let alone climbed up the mountain to the castle that fast? And where had a dragon come from? She'd been on the balcony for, like, five minutes!

Darling sighed again and closed her curtains.

Tomorrow she and her two brothers, Dexter and Daring, would depart for another year at Ever After High. She wandered around her room, looking for something useful to do in preparation, but her trunks had been packed for days. She wouldn't have minded doing the chore herself, but the servants tended to fall all over themselves to help her out in any way. Like, literally fall over themselves. And throw a few punches. One of the groundskeepers gave a guard a black eye in a fight over who got to fold a pair of her socks.

Nothing to do that morning but sit inside and wait until it was time for the Family Ball at her grand-parents' castle. The last Family Ball of the summer was always a big deal.

A sly smile slipped onto Darling's lips. What would they think if she dressed sloppily and didn't brush her hair and generally looked rumpled? She tore open her closet.

The only dress left unpacked was practically a ball gown—it was so shimmery and fancy. *Oh well.* She shrugged it on. But she wouldn't bother to brush her hair. *Ha-ha!* That would cause a scene! Then she glanced at the mirror only to discover her hair already looked brushed and styled and shiny. Why couldn't she achieve the casual rumpled look of her brother, Dexter?

When she heard others shouting that it was time to go, she went to fetch Dexter, though she had to use a secret skill to get them down to the courtyard and the tram on time. Whenever she flipped her hair in a certain way, she could briefly slow time for any who were watching. Her mother said it was because all who saw her couldn't comprehend her stunning beauty and their minds slowed trying to process it. Darling wasn't fond of that explanation, but she wasn't above using the skill in a pinch. Mother didn't approve, but Father didn't like anyone being late. Besides, Dex wouldn't tell on her.

Mother was waiting, a model of posture, poise, and perfection. Any gray in her hair blended with her pale blond locks, sprayed and piled in beehive style. Queen Charming's personal style was kind of stuck a few decades in the past. She reached out, and for a moment Darling thought she was going to give her a hug, but instead she just straightened Darling's ruffle.

"That's better," said her mother. "A Charming princess must always be perfection itself."

"Yes, Mother," said Darling.

Darling climbed into the wobbly tram and stepped close to the windows. She loved traveling at high speeds over the dizzying heights of the valleys and canyons.

"No, no, *you* take a seat, Darling," said her father, King Charming.

"Yes, you and Mother should take them," Daring insisted.

He graciously took her elbow and walked her to one of the plush thrones beside Mother, where she couldn't see the view. Meanwhile, Dexter got to stand right up against the window and enjoy the stomach-plunging pleasure of their swift ride over the abyss. *Lucky Dexter.*

Darling's legs and back cramped. All that energy

inside her was antsy, wiggly, wanting to scream out, so when they finally reached their grandparents' castle, she took Daring's offered hand and swung out of the tram like a monkey.

Mother clucked her tongue.

Darling had heard that sound hundreds of times in her life. It meant, *A Charming princess is ladylike, Darling. You must be ladylike.*

Darling felt her face go hot. She held her hands demurely before her, bowed her head, and didn't speak.

Grandpa Auspicious and Grandma Alluring's home seemed ancient compared with their own bright-as-Daring's-teeth palace. The stones here were gray and brown, weathered, the wind and rain picking interesting shapes into their faces. Inside, the grand ballroom smelled rich and old, carrying remnants of centuries of parties. Darling hadn't yet been in all the rooms. There were so many—large haunting ones, small hidden ones, curved hallways, and secret closets. She looked around, her feet itching to explore.

But there was Mother, watching. And servants, staring at her with marriage proposals they didn't dare speak glistening in their eyes. And her brothers, surrounding her protectively. She wondered if they were even aware how often they did that. *So. Annoying.* And there was a gaggle of her girl cousins, waving her over.

She glanced at Dexter, envying his spot against the wall beside a painting of a flower. She sighed, straightened her shoulders, and joined the princesses.

She'd do her best to play the part she'd inherited at birth of a proper Princess Charming.

After all, she was going back to school tomorrow to start her Legacy Year. She would sign the Storybook of Legends, promise to follow in her mother's footsteps and become a quintessential damsel in distress, claimed by an old, cruel king who wanted her for his bride, trapped, powerless, and then finally saved by a Prince Charming.

Not one of her brother or cousin Charmings, of course. That would be creepy. Fortunately, there seemed to be no end of Prince Charmings in Ever After. Charmings were like rabbits. There were the valley Charmings, the seaside Charmings, and the Charmings of Troll Wood, for example. (The Charmings of Troll Wood had done a lot to civilize local trolls, introducing them to tools like napkins, toothbrushes, and nose-hair clippers.)

"I would like all young ladies to attend me, please!" called out Grandma Alluring. She was dressed in the palest of peach silks, her white hair braided around her head. Her hands were as soft as a baby's skin, but her eyes were steely gray. No one disobeyed Grandma Alluring.

Grandpa Auspicious was gathering the boys for some adventure game. Darling followed Grandma Alluring into the drawing room and took her place on one of the many settees. She looked back over her shoulder at the princes until the door shut.

"My beautiful girls," said Grandma Alluring. "We are going to have some fun today!"

Darling's gaze snapped away from the door. She sat up eagerly.

"We are going to play damsels in distress!" said Grandma.

The princesses squealed with delight.

Darling's shoulders slumped slightly. But not enough for anyone to notice. She had extremely good posture.

"Your grandfather has prepared an exciting

treasure hunt quest for the princes. You will all play a part. Many of the treasures require a special tool or clue the boys can only get by rescuing a princess from a prison."

Between school and family games, Darling had had a lot of waiting-to-be-rescued practice. She sat on the settee perfectly still, ankles crossed, hands loosely clasped, spine straight. But inside, she felt like Cinderella with no fairy godmother.

Grandma Alluring passed around a bowl full of folded pieces of paper. Each princess selected one.

"Ooh, mine says 'highest turret,'" said cousin Caring.

"I got 'cheese cellar,'" said cousin Fragile.

"Blech. 'Pickle barrel.' I hope it's empty at least," said cousin Elegant.

Darling opened her paper. It read, METAL BOX ON EAST ROOF. She snorted a laugh.

"What's funny?" asked cousin Bountiful.

"Oh, nothing." Darling smiled sweetly. Of her family, perhaps only Dexter would laugh with her about how Charmings considered locking yourself in a box on the roof a fun game.

The princesses made their farewells and set off to

shut themselves up in various uncomfortable and lonely places. Darling climbed up and up, finally reaching the highest room on the east side of the castle. She stepped out onto the balcony, and sure enough, there was a metal box secured to the roof.

"Honestly, Grandpa," she whispered.

A little-known fact about damsels: It took great skill and years of practice to put oneself in distress.

Fortunately, Darling had been well trained. She had her Damsel's BFF, an adorable little handbag she kept hooked to her belt. People assumed it held nothing more than a hairbrush and lip gloss. Hardly. She'd converted it from a magical bottom-less bag—a gift from an ogre mage—and stuffed it with handy tools. First and foremost, a princess must be prepared.

Darling rooted around in her bag and pulled out a set of small silver hooks, pinning up her long skirt so it wouldn't drag. She tucked her hair back in a bun. She removed her high heels, stowed them in the bag, and then put on rubber-soled booties and gloves to help her hands and feet grip the slippery roof tiles. Then she ran, leaped, grabbed the roof's edge, and, with her raw upper-body strength, pulled herself up. With practiced balance, she negotiated the steep roof, finally reaching the top.

The walls of the box were made of woven metal strips so at least she would be able see out and breathe, but the fit would be snug. Still, she managed to crawl inside. Something tangly and uncomfortable took up the floor of the box. She started to climb back out to look at it when a strong breeze shut the box's door behind her with a *click*.

She tried to push it open.

Locked tight.

Once again, Darling Charming was left alone with nothing to entertain her but her imagination. She leaned back and through the grate stared at the clouds in the sky. The wind reshaped them slowly before her eyes.

A pirate ship.

A dragon.

A galloping steed.

From the corner of her eye, Darling thought she saw someone. When she sat up, no one was there. Perhaps it had just been a cat running around on the rooftop, but she scanned the roof and the terrace below.

She looked around and spotted movement in the terrace's swimming pool. She narrowed her eyes. Yes, something was definitely swimming in there. Something with a whipping tail and gray scales.

She scooted to one side of the box and examined the uncomfortable thing she was sitting on. It was a net.

Aha. So some prince was supposed to save her in order to get the net and then use it to capture the swimming beast and claim whatever treasure Grandpa Auspicious had dropped into the pool. That was *so* Grandpa.

Darling adjusted her position, trying to get a better look at the pool, and her foot pressed against the locked door. Only it wasn't locked anymore. *Huh.* Maybe she'd been mistaken.

Cautiously, she opened the door, wincing at the whine of its dry hinges. She looked around. No one in sight.

She could sit curled up in a box on a roof for a few hours, waiting for a prince to save her, or...

Darling slid off the roof, grabbing the gutter with one hand as she went over the edge. She dangled for a moment, then dropped the last six feet, taking the fall with bended knees and then a quick back roll, landing on her feet. She padded across the cool blue tiles to the pool and crept to the water's edge.

The breeze rippled the pool into thousands of tiny waves all reflecting the sun, masking whatever swam beneath. She knelt down and peered in—

Jagged-toothed jaws broke the surface of the water. She fell backward, the jaws snapping at the air where her face had been. The beast made a horrid screech and splashed its long, fat tail threateningly. Darling scrambled farther back.

Amateur move, Darling, she scolded herself.

Just because this was a "game" didn't mean her grandfather hadn't put something truly deadly in the pool. Like a razor eel, for example. He expected his grandsons to be wily, strong, and resilient.

And what about his granddaughters?

Darling hooked one corner of the net to a light post at the shallow end of the pool. She waved her hand underwater. The razor eel lashed its tail and swam toward her, its jaws rising out of the water. At the last moment, Darling pulled her hand out, wrapped the net around the eel, and hooked another corner of the net to the post. It was caught, thrashing, making a terrifying squeal.

Darling ran to the deep end of the pool and dived.

Something long and silver shimmered under the blue wash of water. A sword. She tried to swim for it, but it seemed deeper than a sea witch's basement. She lost her breath and came back up.

The razor eel's thrashing and squealing became more desperate. In moments, its razor-sharp fins would slice through the net.

Darling took three quick breaths, inhaled deeply, and dived again. She kicked her legs furiously, swimming straight down. Underwater, the leather hilt of the sword felt smooth and slimy as eel skin. She gripped it with two hands and beat her way to the surface.

A ripple in the water alerted her to the freed eel. She kicked ferociously, paddling with one hand, racing for the edge. Out of the water, the sword felt as heavy as a baby giant. She lifted it onto the pool's side, climbing after it, and felt the air of the eel's exhale on her feet just as she rolled onto the tiled deck.

The eel slapped its tail on the water, splashing

her, enraged to have lost its prey twice. Darling stuck out her tongue.

Wet, shivering, breathless, cold, and messy, she lay on her back and laughed. In the sky, the wind rearranged the clouds, building a knight onto a horse, galloping away.

She heard a sniveling, gasping kind of a cry, and for a moment she thought it was the razor eel, heartbroken that she had beat it. She sat up. No, it was coming from just inside the castle, through the open terrace doors.

She picked up the mammoth sword with two hands and secreted it in a large, decorative urn poolside. She unhooked her skirt, shook out her hair, and pulled her heels out of her Damsel's BFF. She started to wring the water out of her dress, but it was fairymade and already dry. And unwrinkled. A breeze whisked by, drying her hair into perfect, wavy curls. She sighed and rolled her eyes.

Slipping her shoes back on, she tiptoed through the door and found her tiny cousin Good-Enough sitting against the wall, his arms and head resting on his knees, his back shaking with sobs.

His brothers and sisters were named Gallant,

Glorious, Gutsy, Gracious, and Gorgeous, but by the time Good-Enough had come along, his parents had apparently run out of adjectives.

"Hey, Goody," said Darling, crouching beside him. "What's the matter?"

Seeing his older cousin Darling, Good-Enough immediately stood up, fists on hips in a Prince Charming pose that looked only slightly ridiculous on a five-year-old.

"Nothing, fair princess," he said boldly. "I...I just...I can't find anything from the quest, and cousin Errant said I was too little to do it, but I'd thought that maybe if I *did*, then..."

He shrugged. She could see daydreams of a hero's welcome playing behind his eyes before washing away in a new bout of tears.

"I think one of the treasures is hidden out here," said Darling. "Come on!"

She took his hand and led him onto the terrace, Darling carefully keeping herself between him and the pool lest he fall in and meet the razor eel. But he was a quick and keen little boy, and he found the sword in the urn in no time.

Good-Enough's eyes glowed. Even while dragging

the heavy sword back to the ballroom, he couldn't help skipping every few steps.

"Just wait…" he said between huffing breaths. "Just wait…till…Errant…sees me!"

Most of the family had gathered back in the ballroom, princesses saved, princes bearing found treasures, parents beaming at their fairytale-appropriate children.

"Two treasures still undiscovered," Grandpa Auspicious was saying. "The Crochet Hook of Aunt Arachne and the Soaring—"

"Grandpa?" interrupted Darling. Everyone looked at her and she felt her cheeks burn. She ducked her head and started to back out of the room, but her young cousin's eyes looked up at her, bright with excitement.

"Um, Grandpa, may I announce Prince Good-Enough Charming, he who recovered the Soaring Sword of Salamander Steve!"

Everyone turned to look. Darling whispered to Good-Enough, "Swipe the sword in the air."

He could barely lift it with both hands but with one swipe, the sword began to soar, lifting like a helium balloon and carrying Good-Enough with it.

The family cheered, and Good-Enough laughed as he floated over their heads.

Grandpa Auspicious considered the dangling feet of Good-Enough above him as if trying to imagine the lad tangling up a razor eel and dragging a sword out of a pool's depths. Then he turned his attention to Darling and raised an eyebrow.

Darling's breath caught in her throat like a magic fish on a hook. This was her moment. All she had to do was nod. Smile. Let her grandfather know somehow that yes, she had been a hero!

She opened her mouth to speak again.

"Behold the fearless champion!" her brother Daring announced, charging into the ballroom.

He was holding Dexter's hand aloft, for all to see the Crochet Hook of Aunt Arachne in his grip.

Darling swallowed her words and looked down at her feet. Saved by Prince Daring once again. She'd been about to make a huge mistake.

In a few weeks' time, she would sign the Storybook of Legends and promise to live out her mother's story. And all Charming princesses had basically the same story, though from slightly different tales. They weren't supposed to be the rescuing heroes; they were supposed to be the ones needing the rescuing.

No matter that adventure stories sent Darling's heart galloping, that a knight's shiny suit of armor made her *oooh* more than the fanciest ball gown, that her muscles ached to be used, her legs longed to run and leap and climb. She was Darling Charming. And she *must* follow her destiny. All of Ever After knew that refusing to follow their destinies would make their stories and all their characters cease to exist. *Poof!* Gone from Ever After forever after.

No one could know.

Well, except Dexter.

As soon as she could mince her way through the cheering crowd of cousins, she took his arm. She could see more of a story than he was telling dancing in her brother's eyes.

"Charity," he managed to whisper. "And there was a changel—"

He was grabbed by uncles and cousins and hoisted atop shoulders.

A changeling? Darling thought. Changelings were replicas of real people made from carved wood. Once created, they would do *anything* to remain in their stolen guise. But Dexter had used the past-tense verb *was*, so it must no longer be a danger.

"In the dungeon!" he managed to tell her before the crowd carried him away.

Darling nodded, and warmth thrilled through her as she realized, whatever was wrong, her brother trusted her to fix it. She ran down and down into the core of the mountain, where the stairs were hacked out of solid rock. The entrance to the dungeon was marked with two nasty-looking rusty iron spears, but the door was locked. She pulled a small, needle-like hook out of her Damsel's BFF handbag and used the tool to pick the lock. She'd spent enough time locked up in various closets, towers, and boxes in her life to learn a few skills. Sometimes princes were slow about the rescuing and she'd need to get free for a minute and stretch her legs.

Inside, she found cousin Charity just finishing a book.

"Oh, hi, Darling!" said Charity. "Um ... I ... uh ... "

Darling nodded, understanding without an explanation. She wasn't the only princess who sometimes needed a break from being a Charming.

Darling saw there was no cell door, so she ran

back to the entryway, yanked one of the spears from the wall, and hefted it back to Charity's cell.

"Stand back," Darling said, wedging the spear between the bars.

"Okay," Charity said, gathering her things.

Darling pushed the spear with all her strength, and the bars slowly, steadily began to bend. As soon as she'd forced a princess-size gap between the bars, she stopped.

"Can you fit through that?" Darling asked.

"Probably, but I might get my dress dirty," Charity said, frowning.

Darling raised an eyebrow, and then gave the wedged spear a powerful kick. The mortar on the ceiling holding one of the cell bars cracked, the bar itself pulling loose and clattering to the ground. Charity stepped through the gap. She took Darling's hand.

"No one can know," Darling and Charity both said at the same time, and laughed. Charming princesses had more in common than blond hair and button noses.

"You have to read this book. So. Good." Charity thrust a thick tome titled *Dreams of Dogs &*

Lobsters into Darling's hands. "Way worth risking imprisonment-by-changeling."

"Don't you want it?" asked Darling.

"I just finished it. Besides, I've got more." She opened her knapsack, which was stuffed with books: *The De-Viners: Tales of Foliage Removal*, *Why We Woke Up*, and *Beautiful Sneakers*.

"These don't sound terribly exciting," Darling observed.

"Exactly!" said Charity. "Nice, normal stories. Why does everything in this family have to be drama and adventure, magic and glass towers, and who has the most axes in their throwing-ax collection?"

Darling thought she might not mind having a throwing-ax collection herself, but of course she did not say so.

They talked books as they made their way back to the ballroom, about how they loved rereading favorite stories they practically knew by heart as well as discovering new, unexpected ones. They talked about enjoying stories of mystery and heroism as much as quiet books of friendship and family.

The ballroom was boisterous with cousins recounting heroic deeds. Dexter was seated at the head of the dining room table, so long that the servants wore roller skates to more quickly deliver dishes to the far ends.

Darling sat beside Dexter. He handed her a fork and pushed his charmberry-rhubarb pie between them to share. She took a big bite and, turning so only he could see, smiled a red rhubarby smile. Dexter laughed, coughing out crumbs of crust.

No one else would ever know about the razor eel. Or Dexter's defeat of the changeling. But at least Darling knew they were both heroes. That would have to be good enough.

For now.

Lizzie Hearts
(and a)
Home for Hedgehogs

LIZZIE HEARTS SLID A THIN BOOK TITLED *Wonderland! A Libretto of Whimsy* back onto the library shelf. She hadn't enjoyed it. Not at all. It hadn't been a proper book, nor even an improper one. "A bound thing with words" was the fairest description she felt she could give it. And yet, it had *Wonderland* in the title, so she had finished reading those inadequate words nonetheless.

Though to be fair, unless a book about Wonderland managed to transport her back home again, she would always feel that the tome had failed her.

"Off with your head!" she shouted, and the words echoed back at her. The library was empty, most of the students still home for the chapter break. Only she and Kitty Cheshire had remained at Ever After High, having no home to return to.

No home . . . She felt a twinge near her heart. After the Evil Queen poisoned the wild magic of Wonderland, Headmaster Grimm ordered all the doors, portals, and wells to Lizzie's homeland sealed against the infection. Only a few Wonderlandians had escaped, like Madeline Hatter and her father, who now had the Tea Shoppe in Book End. That was where Maddie lived when she wasn't at school. But like Kitty Cheshire, Lizzie was never not at school. There was nowhere else for her to go.

Her finger traced the spines of the books on the shelf looking for another title that had something—*anything*—to do with Wonderland. *Wonderstruck . . . Wonder Princess . . . Wonder Red Now and Other Palindromes* . . . She grabbed an enormous volume titled *Wonderful Wizards, Volume Two: Lands N–Z*, exposing a severed head sitting on the shelf behind it. Lizzie startled and dropped the book onto her foot.

The eyes of the head opened.

"Could you keep it down?" said the head of Kitty Cheshire. "I'm trying to be headless here."

"Ugh," Lizzie said, stomping her foot. "Save the pranks for someone else."

Kitty's head moved out, appearing to float off the shelf and at Lizzie, her eyes wide. Lizzie just rolled her own eyes.

"And put your body back on! Aren't you embarrassed to be walking around like that?"

The rest of Kitty Cheshire brightened into visibility. "It's not really walking if you don't have legs or feet."

"Oh, even if I can't see them, I know what those sneaky feet are doing under there," Lizzie said.

"Under where?" asked Kitty.

"Underwear?"

"Where?"

"In your dresser back at your dorm room, I should hope," said Lizzie.

Kitty giggled, and Lizzie couldn't help laughing a little, too. It was nice that at least one person in Ever After understood her.

"I believe I finished the last Wonderland book in

this inadequate library," Lizzie said. "I am therefore bored. Croquet?"

At the mention of the sport, Lizzie's pet hedgehog, Shuffle, popped her head out of Lizzie's handbag.

"*Roink?*" she grunted.

"In a minute, poppet," Lizzie said, patting the wee spiky head.

"Croquet again?" Kitty said. "Meh."

"Don't say 'meh,'" Lizzie said. "It's unbecoming."

"Myeh," Kitty tried out instead.

"Better, but now I don't know what you mean." Lizzie picked up her handbag and walking scepter and began muttering under her breath. "*Myeh*... nonsense, and not the right kind of nonsense, not the kind of nonsense that makes good, solid sense. Come along, then, Kitty."

"I think I'll just stay here for a while. In the library," Kitty said from atop a bookcase. "Curl up with a good book."

Lizzie turned back. "Really?"

"Rlyeh," Kitty said, pieces of her fading away until only her mouth remained. "And also fhtagn," the mouth said, and then vanished completely.

"Well, I never!" Lizzie shouted at the air. She

had no idea what a "fhtagn" was, but it sounded rude. She waited a moment in case Kitty changed her mind and reappeared with a croquet mallet. She didn't.

"Fine," Lizzie said, stomping out of the library. "I will have fun by myself!"

Lizzie marched out the doors of the library, scepter held high. She kept right on marching, as if leading an army to battle, all the way out of the school and toward the croquet field.

She passed a little man raking leaves, one of Ever After High's gardeners. Kitty had told her that all the groundskeepers were part of Old Tom Thumb's family and were usually too small to notice. Though little, this man was far larger than a thumb. Besides, it was Kitty's nature to be misleading. Lizzie suspected he had considerably more leprechaun than Thumb in his family tree. Besides, the name stitched on his coveralls read GREEN.

He eyed her as she marched onto the croquet lawn.

"Croquet!" Lizzie announced to the grass.

Green startled, dropping his rake.

"Um… what ye say?" he asked in a high, squeaky voice.

"I said *croquet*!" Lizzie answered.

Green did not seem consoled by this clarification. His eyes darted around as if afraid others were about to run up and yell things at the grass, too. Hesitantly, he raised a hand and gestured toward the small garden shed. That was where the mallets and hoops were stored, so she pointed that out to him.

"*That is where the mallets and hoops are stored!*" she shouted.

Green nodded and started to rake again, still staring at her as if she was the odd one instead of the only person around who was helpfully shouting "Croquet!"

In Wonderland, a clutch of card soldiers would have set up the croquet court, but in Ever After, Lizzie had to do it herself. She placed the hoops in properly awkward locations, skirting the grove of invisible trees that had sprouted on the lawn. No way to cut them down until someone found an invisible ax, which was, she had been told, impossible. *Ha!* Nothing *is impossible.*

Even returning home again? she dared to ask herself. But the thought prompted sniffles in her nose and wetness in her eyes—*Probably just allergies*—so she ignored it.

Lizzie dug the hazard troughs, politely invited all the grass-dwelling insects to take their business elsewhere, and even managed a fairly good swamp wicket by dumping buckets of water into a hollow.

Proud of her work, she plopped Shuffle onto the grass. The Wonderland-bred hedgehog promptly curled up into a nearly indestructible ball, and Lizzie whacked her with a flamingo mallet. The hedgehog sailed through the first hoop, rebounded on a second, and settled just on the edge of one of the hazard troughs.

"Good enough," Lizzie said, hands on her hips. "Your turn."

She waited for the sound of a mallet striking one of the inferior Ever After croquet balls, but it never came. She whirled, a mouth full of insults about insufferably slow players, only then remembering she didn't actually have anyone to play with.

Green was still eyeing her nervously. He was standing beside a huge pile of leaves and holding a long stick with a tiny flame on the end, like a thin, fully grown birthday candle. He dipped the flaming stick onto the leaves, catching them on fire.

"Oh, for Queen's sake!" Lizzie said.

She grabbed the still half-full bucket and sped toward the gardener.

Green made a terrified squawk and ran away, looking over his shoulder with wide eyes as if afraid she would chase him.

But Lizzie made straight for the burning leaves. She tossed the water from the bucket, extinguishing the fire.

"By the vorpal sword, what is the matter with you?" she yelled.

Green whimpered and kept running.

Lizzie huffed, stalking back to the garden shed, picking up all the hoops as she went. She tossed them unceremoniously into the garden shed. A moment later she huffed impatiently and returned to put it all away properly.

♥

Everything has a place and should be put in it. That will be your job, since people, things, and in-betweens tend to forget their place.

♥

It was one of several special messages her mother had written for her on a pack of playing cards. The cards were full of advice and not-advice, instructions and out-structions, as well as the occasional verbal sneeze. She pulled the deck out of her pocket, her thumb running over the word *Lizzie* her mother had inscribed on the case.

Everything has a place.... Except Lizzie Hearts, perhaps. She could put the croquet hoops back in the shed but not herself back in Wonderland.

"*Roink?*" Shuffle noised, snuffling at Lizzie's boot.

"What's that, Shuffle?" Lizzie whispered. "You need a place to call your own? Come on, let's go play cards."

During the chapter break at Ever After High, one could circle the school grounds and not run into a single person. Lizzie rarely used the benches along the paths. Benches seemed to invite sharing a seat with others. Lizzie was not a fan.

But there was one particular bench in a particular place that Lizzie could usually depend on keeping to herself. Only today, that very bench was occupied.

"I arrived just after you," said Mrs. Her Majesty the White Queen.

Lizzie supposed she meant "before you," but time played with the White Queen's mind like a kitten with a ball of yarn.

The tall, pale teacher patted the unoccupied portion of the bench beside her. Lizzie sat. One did not ignore an invitation from the White Queen.

The bench topped a hillock overlooking the wishing well that used to lead to Wonderland. Now it was just a regular, nontraveling well with unkempt, wild plants tangling around its base. Lizzie *tsk*ed her tongue. Something so precious should not be in disrepair. Still, the plants themselves lightened her heart. They were Wonderland plants! The only ones in Ever After. She'd transplanted some in pots to put in her dorm room, but those always withered and wilted. The Wonderland plants only seemed to thrive near the well.

"My palace would normally only be a year away," the White Queen said, gesturing at the neglected well. "But the halfwise backtime in which I prefer to walk doesn't slide that direction here. Not in Ever After."

Lizzie nodded. Back home, all one had to do to understand the White Queen was to imagine oneself living backward. Thursday after Friday, August after September, breakfast after lunch. But in Ever After, things worked differently. Sometimes the White Queen ate breakfast in the morning like everyone else. It was confusing to everyone, including the queen.

"Less than a year for you, though," the White Queen said, smiling at Lizzie.

Lizzie's heart had jumped. Did she mean in less than a year she'd be going home?

"Before you're signed into the book of destiny, that is," said the White Queen. "It is your Legacy Year."

Lizzie frowned. The White Queen was talking about signing the Storybook of Legends. Lizzie's destiny was to claim the Card Castle throne as the next Queen of Hearts of Wonderland. But now…She looked at the overgrown well, wild plants scattered around it, untended. She was exiled from Wonderland—how could she possibly fulfill her destiny? Everyone knew that if you didn't sign the Storybook of Legends and relive your parent's story, you and your story would go *poof*. Would Lizzie vanish, too, if she couldn't get home? If she had no home? No kingdom to rule? It didn't seem fair.

"It will all work out, sweetheart," the White Queen said, patting Lizzie on the knee. It was an unexpected kindness, unexpectedly clear-spoken.

The queen stood. "Stay here for a while. Build something."

"Okay," Lizzie said, and watched the White Queen glide away.

Shuffle nosed out of Lizzie's handbag. "Sorry, little one," Lizzie said, taking her hedgehog out of the bag and placing her carefully on the bench. "I'll build something for you. Your own place."

Lizzie shuffled a fresh deck of playing cards and shook her head at the mess of foliage surrounding the Wonderland well. In her mother's Card Kingdom, every plant was nurtured, every flower painted. Surely someone's head would come off for allowing a well to be so neglected, its plants so overgrown and rebellious.

Lizzie placed two cards, leaning against each other, on the seat of the bench. Then another, and another. In no time, she was placing the last of her cards on the top of a surprisingly accurate re-creation of the Ever After High girls' dorms.

"That's your room there," Lizzie said, pointing to

one of the rooms on an upper floor of the construction. "It's the same one I stay in. You know, in the real building."

Shuffle sniffed at the cards and then skittered into the card building, which had no trouble supporting her weight. Lizzie was fairy, fairy good at building things with cards. Shuffle climbed up the card stairs, and settled into the room Lizzie had said was hers.

"It isn't really to scale," Lizzie said apologetically. It was a tone of voice she reserved only for Shuffle and a few plants she thought deserved respect. "At least, not hedgehog-scale."

"*Roink*," said Shuffle, looking nervously at the card walls closing her in.

"Too cramped? And lonely, I suspect, in that big house, so far from your real home, so few friends who understand your wee little *roink*s and adorable little sniffles..."

Shuffle scampered down and onto Lizzie's lap. She plucked a corner card from the building, and it collapsed.

As she gathered the cards together, she was struck with an unsettling memory of a time in Wonderland when lightning had struck the Card barracks and it burned to the ground. Those soldiers had been so despondent when waiting for the barracks to be rebuilt, with no place to call home.

What had brought that to mind? She sniffed and smelled real smoke.

That fool of a gardener had lit the piles of leaves on fire again and was just standing nearby, watching them burn.

Lizzie ran down the hill to the Wonderland Well, weaving her cards together as someone might use reeds to make a basket. By the time she reached the well, she had a serviceable card-bucket. She dumped the bucket into the well, filling it to the brim with water.

Lizzie flew past Green and flung the contents of her emergency card-bucket at the fire. The water scattered beautifully and the flames guttered out with a hiss.

"Stop it!" Lizzie shouted at the gardener. "Are you insane?"

She had opted to use the word *insane*, because this fire-starting Ever Afterling didn't deserve the honor of being called mad.

"Nae, ye stop it," Green said, even as he backed away from her, his hands gripping each other. "I's trying to burnna leafs. It's me job to burnna pile o' leafs."

"Is it your job to murder innocent little hedgehogs, too?"

"Hedgie-hoggies?" he asked, his nose wrinkled, head tilted.

Lizzie sighed loudly and dug into the wet, slightly singed leaves, finally exposing a gray-spined, pink-nosed hedgehog blinking at the light.

"A hedgie-hoggie!" said the gardener.

"Honest to nonsense," said Lizzie, "I almost think everyone in Ever After has to actually see a hedgehog to know it was there. I almost assume you weren't capable of sensing that this pile of leaves was home to an entire family."

And she brushed aside more clumpy, smoking leaves, revealing seven little hedgehogs, a bit ashy and a lot frightened.

"*Roink?*" said Shuffle, nuzzling them one by one.

"Nae, nae, mum!" said Green, more frightened than ever. "I...I did nae know they was there! Honest to...uh, nonsense."

"What is your name?" Lizzie asked. "I need to report this malfeasance to someone!"

"Green, mum," he said, pointing to his name tag. "Green Thumb. But dinnae be malfeasing. I fae an sure love hedgie-hoggies all. I'd nae be hurtin em!"

Lizzie snorted. "If it was an honest mistake, then why are you trembly and wombly and sniffly, *hm*?"

"If'n you d'nae mind me saying, mum, you're scary!"

Lizzie nodded. A highly appropriate answer. Her mother would be pleased. She thought of the advice the Queen of Hearts had written on one of the cards.

♥

It is better to be gloved than bearded, and better to be fearded than loved.

♥

Lizzie was inclined to believe this Green Thumb. Anyone with enough sense to fear her could only be honest. She was frankly more surprised to find that Kitty hadn't been misleading her about the Thumbs after all.

She crouched down to the group of bedraggled hedgehogs. They were Ever After hedgehogs, not Wonderland ones, so they didn't seem to recognize her, since they didn't bow or anything. She chose not to be offended.

"Hey, little guys. I'm Lizzie Hearts, and I'm going to find you a better place to live. Everyone deserves a little place of their own. Follow me."

Lizzie, Shuffle, and all eight hedgehogs marched in an indignant line past the gardener. Lizzie started toward the bench, thinking to build them a card palace, but she caught a whiff of wild fluxberry blossoms and veered toward the old Wonderland wishing well. Even being near the well, wading knee-deep through the tangles of overgrown Wonderlandian plants, Lizzie Hearts just felt right. Better. Beamish and unbefuddled. Surely the hedgehogs would thrive here.

And indeed, the refugee hedgehogs immediately scurried into a fluxberry bush and nestled under its glossy green leaves. Above them, the ever-changing fluxberries glowed slightly like disco lights, fading from pink to purple to orange.

"Mayhap ye build a home here," Green Thumb said behind her.

Lizzie looked at him with as good a grump-eye as she could manage.

"Are you implying that *I* need a home?" said Lizzie. "Are you trying to say that I'm obsessed with the hedgehogs' home because I, too, am feeling homeless and am empathizing with their displacement as some sort of metaphor for my own? That would be highly inappropriate on your part!"

"No, no, for'n the hedge-hoggies, mum," he said. "They's seeming to cuzzle and nuddle the Wonder plants."

A couple of the little creatures had emerged from the fluxberry bush and were nibbling tufts of nodgrass.

"But if'n ye's keen on makin a garden here, I'd be on helping, too, should ye…"

"No!" Lizzie snapped, and then felt bad about it when the little man startled backward. "I mean," she said more calmly, "it is a good idea, but I would like to do it alone."

Green nodded. "For'n fer certain, mum. But feel ye free to use me tools, aye?"

"Off with your head," she said, and then mumbled, "and by that, I mean thank you."

The hedgehogs scuttled about the wild plants, eating, hiding, squeaking. Shuffle went from hedgehog to hedgehog, touching noses and sniffling politely. It *was* a good idea the gardener had helped her to have. A little Wonderland garden, properly tended, would be the perfect habitat for any hedgehog, be they Ever After or Wonderland.

She dusted herself off and started back to the school. She would need a book on caring for hedgehogs. She did perfectly well with Shuffle, but she, like most Wonderland hedgehogs, was fairly self-sufficient. Perhaps Shuffle's companionship and the eating of Wonderland plants would even turn the ordinary hedgehogs into Wonder hoggies like Shuffle.

But turning a wild grove into an orderly one? Lizzie might need some tips on where to begin. She couldn't very well talk to her mother about it, so it was back to the library for her, though she doubted such a helpish and unlikely book existed.

And yet, the moment she walked into the library, a book fell off the shelf and onto her shoe for the second time that day.

"Shoe!" Lizzie shouted at her foot. "Cease this book-baiting at once!"

She picked up the book: *Hedgehog Husbandry and*

the Ordering of Wild Groves. Well. What a perfectly appropriate book for her quest.

Lizzie smiled. Suddenly she didn't feel so lost, so forgotten. Suddenly she felt a little more like the Princess of Hearts and a lot more hopeful. Her destiny wasn't impossible, because nothing was. Home was far away, but there were ways to bring it closer. Even if just a teeny-weeny-bleeny bit.

She really didn't know what the gardener was going on about, accusing *her* of being lonely and needing the Wonderlandish home for herself. But quietly, secretly, the Princess of Hearts's heart beat a little more hopefully at the thought of a Wonderland garden, even a small one for hedgehogs.

Lizzie heard a yawn. There was Kitty, curled up on the bookcase exactly where she had left her hours ago.

"Kitty, have you been napping there this whole day?" Lizzie asked.

Kitty examined her nails. "More or less. Hey, you want to get something to eat? The Castleteria kitchen might be open."

"Yes!" Lizzie said, slamming the book shut and stuffing it into her bag. "We shall eat!"

"As you wish, Your Highness," Kitty said with her customary grin.

Lizzie nodded, but she couldn't help looking at her friend sideways. Kitty's grin always made Lizzie wonder what Kitty was up to.

And wonder was a marvelous thing.

From the Desk of
Lizzie Hearts

Secrets are secrets
and cannot be told.
If anyone tells you a secret,
they are lying.
If anyone tells you a lie,
they might be secreting.
In either case, step away.
Lies and secretions are
to be avoided.

To succeed in life
as a queen and princess,
you need four things in your
brain and two in your pocket.
The pocket things are solid,
and the brain things are not.
Be sure not to mix them up.

Puddles are the thing
you think is the thing,
but is really the top
of the thing,
and the bottom
makes you drown.

Hair hides skin,
but hide can also be skin,
especially if you
have four legs.
Count your legs and
comb your hair.

Depending on
where you live,
a boot can be a foot case,
a trunk case, or a preposition.
Be sure you know where you
are before getting dressed.
When in doubt,
go barefoot.

Never believe a lie.
Unless it's the truth—
then go right ahead.

Fish love to be confused.
Tell a fish a riddle today
that has no answer.

Clouds are well and fine
up in the sky,
but never let one
into your mind.
Not even if it says "Please."

Tomatoes are sneaky.
They love to trick you
into believing
they are strawberries
or cherries or apples.
Before taking a bite,
point at the thing and declare,
"You are a tomato!"
That'll show 'em!

Yelling "Off with your
head!" is a lot more fun
than actually
following through.
Invest time in more
pleasant pursuits,
like croquet and
competitive eating.

Kitty Cheshire (and the) Tricksy Day[1]

[1] Pardon this highly unusual footnote, but I must break the Narrator's "fourth wall" to explain that this story will be "tricksy" in more than one way. Kitty Cheshire does not like being narrated. She seems to be aware of my watching her, and she resists. At times her thoughts and feelings squirm away from my inspection. I shall do my best, however, to narrate a completely true story about Ever After's most elusive character.

A SUMMER AT EVER AFTER HIGH HAD ITS advantages. Kitty Cheshire and Lizzie Hearts had free run of the castle, with only Mrs. Her Majesty the White Queen as chaperone. And the White Queen's idea of chaperoning was to meet the two girls before breakfast, challenge them to "think of six impossible things—quick! Be quick," and then leave them alone for the rest of the day.

Freedom!

She and Lizzie played endless rounds of croquet,

shopped in Book End, and spent teatime[2] with Madeline Hatter at her father's Tea Shoppe. But after two months, Kitty had the unreasonable urge to actually see some of their other Ever After High friends. It was nonsense, surely! Lizzie and Maddie were by far the least annoying people she knew.[3]

But still, when Kitty thought of all her classmates returning tomorrow to start their Legacy Year, she actually felt relieved.

Tomorrow. Kitty stretched out on a library bookcase and felt exhausted by the idea of having to wait till tomorrow. And whenever boredom inched into Kitty, she began to get ticklish in her tricksy brain, impatient in her impudent toes, and she generally all around craved for chaos.

"I believe I finished the last Wonderland book in this inadequate library," Lizzie was saying. "I am therefore bored. Croquet?"

---

[2] The Mad Hatter's Haberdashery & Tea Shoppe defines teatime as "any hour upon which a clock might point a hand at a number—unless the clock has no numbers, or no hands, which is an alarming thing, and a case of alarms can only be cured by sitting down immediately with a cup of tea and perhaps a cookie."

[3] Here, for example, Kitty was blocking me from her thoughts and feelings so I had to guess by her actions and expressions. I may be wrong. Perhaps she just had gas.

"I think I'll just stay here for a while," said Kitty. "In the library. Curl up with a good book."[4]

After Lizzie left, Kitty examined her nails. Fluffed her hair. Yawned with teeth exposed.

"I am bored," Kitty said aloud.

"Bored," she repeated.

"Bored bored bored. Boooored. Booooo. Boogie. Beauregard. Banana squash."[5]

She nodded and said it again. "Banana squash."

But even with such fantastic words as *banana squash* to entertain her, boredom still nipped at her heels. Living in this school all summer felt far too much like being in a cage.

"Cats don't like cages," she said to the library. "Or bubble baths. Or empty sardine cans."

Silence. Kitty wrinkled her nose.[6]

So Kitty blinked and disappeared.

She was In-Between. Though now she was

---

[4] I am sorry to say that Kitty is being misleading. She does that sometimes.

[5] I believe that Kitty is fond of the sound of her own voice. Each day, she speaks strings of words till she stumbles upon her favorite. Today it is *banana squash*. Yesterday it was *popcorn*. Past favorites include *elbow*, *haberdashery*, *inventory*, and *cantaloupe*. Try saying them aloud. They really are delightful words.

[6] I believe here she was expecting the library to respond, and when it didn't, she felt insulted.

invisible to the world, the world was not invisible to her. The library was still there, though faded, gray, and wispy, as if everything were underwater.

She could move so much more quickly In-Between, with no troublesome people or furniture or reality to get in her way. In one step, she reached the far end of the library. Another, and she passed through the wall into the gray trembling shadow of the outside world.

If the sun blazed in the sky, she could spot no sign of it here. There were no shadows In-Between—or rather, everything was shadows. And Kitty raced through the shadows of the Real quicker than a jub-jub bird flits after a lemon meringue pie.

Kitty poked her head into the Mad Hatter's Tea Shoppe to see what chaos she could cause, but then laughed at herself. What more chaos could she bring into a shop where every surface was covered in doors, teapots flew to you, and coffee cake coughed? Actually, bringing "order" into the Mad Hatter's shop would be funnier than "chaos," and order definitely wasn't Kitty's thing.

The Mad Hatter ran from the kitchen, walked right up to where Kitty's invisible head was poking into the shop, and shouted, "No room! No room!"[7] His words were wobbly and watery, the way she heard all real-world sounds that drizzled into In-Between.

Kitty stuck out her tongue at him and pulled her head back through the wall.

A very ordinary-looking girl was walking down the street—every hair smoothed into place, her gray clothing perfectly ironed, her posture so stiff her vertebrae must fear her to stay so solidly in line. Clearly a new student arriving at Ever After High from some kingdom far, far away. Kitty giggled. Ordinary people were hilarious! And also a hex-cellent way to introduce some riddle-diculous order into chaos...

Kitty appeared behind the girl and tapped her shoulder. "Hello."

The girl turned, taking a step back. "Oh! Do I know you? Um...I am Clara Lear."[8]

"I am...a helper," said Kitty with her customary

---

[7] The Mad Hatter couldn't really see her. No one can see Kitty when she was In-Between. But he was just mad enough to think he could, which turns out is very nearly the same thing.

[8] You may recognize this name if you read Madeline Hatter's story, which I narrated previously in this fine volume.

smile. "An official Book End helper. What can I help you find? 'Cause I'm so helpy like that."

The girl sighed. "Everything here seems to be inside out and backward! Not at all nice and neat like home. I just need someplace normal and quiet, where I can sit down and rest without any unpleasant surprises."

Kitty's smile widened. "No place more ordinary, regular, and surprise-free than the Tea Shoppe on the corner!"

"Thank you, Book End helper," said Clara Lear. Posture perfectly perfect, she marched into the Tea Shoppe.

Kitty hung around a moment to see what kind of mischief she'd caused by introducing an ordinary girl into an extraordinary shop. But her nose began to twitch, her toes wiggled, and a moment later, Kitty disappeared.[9]

She leaped around the In-Between version of Book End, passing through the walls of shops, and dived headfirst into the Book End wishing well.

---

[9] This happens a lot to Kitty. She sets up clever pranks and uncomfortable tricks but can't quite manage to stick around long enough to see what happens. I believe she is plagued with boredom.

Traveling by wishing well while In-Between was a roll of the dice. She never knew where she'd end up, but wherever it was, she'd get there faster than a mome rath squeak.

She popped out of the well as dry as a shadow. Moving around In-Between was a bit like running, a little like dreaming, and a lot like swimming. She kicked her legs in the gray sunless, airless shadow world and swam above the treetops to get high and spy out her location.[10] Ah-ha, there was Sleeping Beauty Palace!

Purr-fect.

Kitty continued her dry, airy swim to the third floor of the palace and peeked into a window. Briar Beauty was still asleep in bed. No surprise.[11] Open trunks hinted that she would be spending the day packing for school. Now, how to cause the most mischief?

Kitty appeared back in the Real, and colors filled the room, mostly shades of pink. She began to poke

---

[10] If it were appropriate, I would tell you that I wish I could do this, too.

[11] From her frequent naps, you might assume Briar Beauty loved to sleep. Just the opposite. She stayed up as late as she could every night to avoid it and so was under-slept and apt to nap all day. Because her mother also has frequent and random naps, some assume it's a hereditary sleep condition. But perhaps her mother is simply exhausted. She is, after all, mother to eight young sons.

around. A hot-pink, rose-embossed diary lay on the bedside table. Kitty flipped through it, hoping for some highly silly princess gossip she could use for chaos-causing.[12] But Briar had simply jotted down pages and pages of party ideas, like *Book-to-School Party* and *Legacy Day Dance*. Some entries, like *Litter Awareness Luncheon* and *The Pretend-You-Are-a-Duck Party*, made it clear that Briar could turn any event into a spellebration.

Beneath Briar's bed was a chest full of jewelry. Ah-ha! The school's number one fashionista would pop like a glitter bomb if all her precious accessories disappeared. A hexcellent prank. Kitty was no cat burglar; she wouldn't steal anything. But to simply relocate…

Kitty carefully opened the chest, filled her hands with the jewelry, and disappeared. She let herself sink through two floors and speed-skipped down a corridor, following voices into the ballroom.

The hardwood floor, polished smooth by centuries of dancers, was cluttered now with chairs, stools, and coatracks, all draped with white bedsheets.

---

[12] At least, I think that's what she was doing. When I tried to peer closer at her to see inside her thoughts, she hissed as if she could sense me.

"Mom said not to take the silk sheets off her bed anymore," Kitty heard one little Beauty brother say from somewhere inside the massive fort.

"Yeah, but she's asleep," said another. "Probably."

Yes, this would do. Kitty reappeared just long enough to place the jewelry in the center of the room and promptly vanished.

A few moments later, she heard a Beauty princeling cry, "Treasure!"

"Treasure? Let's play pirates!"

"Yo ho ho!"

Kitty snickered. *Chaos! Sweet, sweet chaos!* This was her destiny, to follow in her mother's footsteps and become the next riddling, teasing trickster of Wonderland, the fablelous Cheshire Cat. And after such a ho-hum-drum summer, she could definitely use more tricksy practice. After all, she was just weeks away from signing the Storybook of Legends and committing to her destiny.[13]

A few leaps and a dive later, Kitty hopped out of another wishing well into another kingdom. Kitty wiggled, sighed, and popped back into the Real.

---

[13] At least, I assume she was eager to become more like her mother. After all, they are very much alike.

Spending too much time In-Between made her feel shivery and odd, as if she were made of rubber.[14]

So Kitty walked from the wishing well along a lane toward a large, many-spired castle. A group of villagers were skipping along.

"Hello there," Kitty said with an unsettling smile. "Can you tell me where we are?"

"Why, the most perfect kingdom in all of Ever After!" said a round-cheeked, dimpled little girl.

Kitty noticed the I ♥ APPLE T-shirts and buttons.

"Ah-ha," said Kitty.

That must be White Castle up ahead. Her unsettling smile settled.

"I love living here," said a redheaded young man.

"Me too," said a twinkly-eyed old man.

The villagers all sighed in unison and continued on their way.[15]

———❤———

[14] A Cheshire family legend tells of Kitty's great-great-uncle who spent so much time In-Between that he returned to the Real as no more than a shadow. He still managed to play excellent tricks, however, by merging with other people's shadows on the pavement and then suddenly putting his shadow hands on his shadow head in silly gestures. He frightened so many card soldiers they shuffled themselves.

[15] The popular magazine *EAH Weekly* named Snow White's kingdom "The Sighingest Kingdom in the Land, But in a Good Way."

Bunnies and robins hopped across the lane. Elegantly dressed dwarves gathered flowers, humming to themselves. The breeze was just strong enough to rustle the tree branches, sending white blossoms raining down like confetti.

Kitty entered the castle courtyard and spied Apple White making a fond farewell to her parents and climbing into the fanciest, most enor-malous hybrid carriage Kitty had ever seen. Seriously, you could fit, like, a hundred clowns in there, or at least twenty normal people.

Kitty disappeared, swam inside the carriage just as Apple climbed in, and squeezed between the shadows of two servants.

The servants were talking about Apple White's beauty.

"Just look at her eyes, her skin," whispered a maid.

Apple's pale cheeks blushed. Clearly she was overhearing everything.

Let's see, how to push the Fairest of the Halls' buttons?

"So beautiful," said another servant. "The *perfect* Snow White."

Kitty let just her smile appear, there in the back of the carriage, where no one could see it.

"Well, except for the hair," Kitty's mouth whispered. "A shame she was born blond."

She disappeared her mouth quickly before she laughed out loud. She did backward somersaults, laughing out loud in the shadow world as the hybrid carriage drove on.

Kitty leaped and floated through Apple's home, occasionally allowing her hand to appear in the Real in order to knock over a vase, rearrange throw pillows, or leave fingerprint trails on otherwise spotless windows.

She shadow-sneaked up to Apple's room, giggling over plans to hide Apple's One Reflection action-figure collection. But Apple's bedroom wasn't empty.

Snow White was sitting on the edge of her daughter's bed. She picked up a pillow, held it to her face as if breathing in the scent, and then hugged it to her chest.

Snow White's sad eyes and slow exhale stopped Kitty. She squirmed, uncomfortable. And then she left.[16]

---

[16] Snow White was unsuspecting, vulnerable, and just prime for a prank. So why didn't Kitty play a trick on her? Is Kitty more sensitive than we assume? Perhaps Apple's mother reminded Kitty of her own?

On to another wishing well. This one spit her out on a mountaintop, the courtyard of an ancient and impressive castle. She passed through the walls and inside to a humongous ballroom. A plethora of mostly blond, tall, graceful people laughed and talked and ate and danced.[17]

The Charming Family Ball! Kitty snickered, an amused hiss.

Like the Whites, these Charming folk were obsessed with cleanliness. Kitty float-spun to a garden on the mountainside courtyard. She slipped into the Real to stomp around in a plant bed, smearing her shoes with dirt. Then she popped back into an empty hallway. She was walking along, snickering and leaving her dirty footprints all over their nice, clean floor, when she sniffed something unusual. Kitty followed the scent to a closet.

A changeling! She detected the most definite

---

[17] It is an interesting note about Kitty's character that she was mostly unaffected by this sight. Upon first entering a room full of Charmings, people have been known to collapse to the floor, weeping for the beauty. Only ogres and half-ogre servants have proven robust enough to work at Charming Family Balls without breaking down, though even they get weak-kneed and apt-to-propose when face-to-face with Darling Charming.

sawdusty tang of a changeling.[18] What in Ever After was a changeling doing at a Charming Family Ball? Kitty popped into the closet, nothing visible but her eyes, and spotted a yellow-eyed changeling sitting in the dark and dressed in the disguise of a Charming princess. The yellow eyes looked right at her own.

"What issss here?" the changeling hissed.

Gulping, Kitty disappeared her eyes, too. Even In-Between, her heart beat harder. Her fingers twitched, wanting to stay and see what might happen next. But her shadow legs shivered, wanting to move on. Even invisible, Kitty didn't feel quite safe so close to a changeling.[19]

She swam-ran her way up and reappeared on the roof. There seemed to be no higher spot in all the world than a mountaintop Charming castle.

Kitty took a deep breath and shouted, "Banana squash!"

---

[18] If I was correctly interpreting Kitty's actions here, then she has a most remarkable sense of smell! Hmm, I wonder if Narrators have a scent she can detect....

[19] I rarely see Kitty show any signs of fear. The changeling made her more uncomfortable than afraid, I believe. But one time, when I merely narrated the word *Jabberwock*, Kitty went invisible and didn't reappear for hours.

Kitty ran and leaped about, from chimney to roof rail, taking full advantage of her fantastic Cheshire balance. The freedom was exhilarating. And if she ever happened to slip (*ha!*) she could always just pop into In-Between before she fell far enough to hurt herself.

As soon as she'd been old enough to walk, her mother had taken her to the Tumtum Grove in Wonderland, together leaping from treetop to treetop. Now, racing along the ridgepole of the Charming palace roof, she looked behind her, half expecting to see her mother there, grinning and chasing after her, laughing into the sky.[20]

"Run, Kitty, run!" her mother would say. "Make them chase you and never catch you. You are a Cheshire, my riddle-icious kitten. You are the wind itself!"

The spicy scent of Tumtum resin seemed to fill Kitty's nostrils. She threw back her head and laughed.

"They can chase all they want, Mother," Kitty called out. "I am a Cheshire!"

[20] Kitty was so distracted and happy here that she accidentally let this memory slip out where I could see it. What a lovely morsel.

A smell caught Kitty's attention, yanking her thoughts back to the present. The scent of someone she knew, but up on the roof?

Curiosity had never hurt Kitty. She crept along, her feet silent on the roof tiles, following the peachy, creamy smell. By Humpty Dumpty's shell, it was Darling Charming! Locked up in a metal box on the roof! Honestly, and people said that Wonderland-ians were weird.

Kitty had spied on enough Charming family events to guess what was going on—Darling was waiting to be rescued. Talk about scratch-out-your-eyeballs boring.

Keeping invisible, Kitty crept closer. Her hand appeared in the Real, unlatching the box's door from the outside. Darling seemed to hear her and looked up, but Kitty disappeared her hand again and leaped away, running along the In-Between rooftops, leaping over chimneys, and laughing in the wind. Darling clearly loved waiting in roof boxes. Would she stay in the unlocked box? Would she cry that her precious rescuing game was ruined?[21]

---

[21] Of course, you, dear reader, already know Darling's reaction, as you read her story earlier in this outstanding volume of tales.

Kitty's feet still longed to keep moving, keep moving, so she didn't stick around to see the hilarity unfold.

Another wishing well later, Kitty crouched on the roof of a café, watching Cedar Wood sniffle at flowers and generally look waifish and homesick, even though she was still home.

Kitty yawned hugely, all her teeth exposed. How imploringly, roaringly boring this all was.

But then a giantish boy with skinny fingers started pointing them at Cedar and making a hullabaloo and fussy-fuss.

"Tell us what it's like to be a fake puppet girl?" he said in rudish, brutish tones.

Kitty wouldn't say that Cedar Wood was her friend. Did Kitty have friends to speak of? She stopped to consider but got bored with the thought and, yawning, decided to think about cheese instead.[22]

Her cheese reverie was interrupted by that tall boy mean-wording Cedar again.

---

[22] This was fairly simple to guess, even with Kitty hiding her thoughts from me. Whenever she licks her lips and looks up, she's thinking about cheese.

"Tell us more, Cedar Wood! What are you most scared of?"

And Cedar ran away, sniveling and sad-ish. Cedar, who last year went into the Castleteria kitchen herself and made a mug of cinnamon milk for Kitty when she'd had a cold.

Well. If Kitty did have a friend…it was Lizzie Hearts. And Madeline Hatter. But besides them, she'd say it was almost Cedar Wood. And no one, not even towering boys with skinny fingers, messes with one of Kitty Cheshire's almost-friends![23]

Time for some lesson-teaching, that's what, tut-tut.

Kitty hung off the roof right behind the boys, allowing just her mouth to reappear. She whispered, "Dare you to go swimming."

"What?" said the taller boy. "You dare me to do what?"

"I didn't say anything," said the shorter boy.

"Dare you to go swimming right now," Kitty whispered.

"What, you don't think I don't know how to swim or something?" The taller boy threw his towel over

---

[23] Some might consider being Kitty Cheshire's "almost-friend" a high honor indeed.

his shoulder and stalked off, muttering, "I'll show you."

Kitty's mouth snickered. By the piles of empty plates on their table, these boys had eaten a king's ransom worth of sweets. Everyone knew that swimming right after overeating would give them a terrible stomachache.[24] Well, that's just what he deserved for being bullyish and nasty-eyed at Cedar Wood.

Despite her recent victory, the cutesy seaside village bored Kitty, so she ran through the shadow world, zooming faster than a falcon flies, and tumbled headfirst down another wishing well.

No town, no palace nearby that Kitty could see. She popped into the Real and spun around in the fragrant woods, sunlight filtering through the round aspen leaves, brightening the soft needles of the evergreens. Animals crept out of sight, but to Kitty their scents were as clear as road signs.

And now a human scent.

Sniffing her way, Kitty tracked down a farmer wandering through the woods. He tiptoed, his eyes

---

[24] I don't think everyone knows this, but Kitty believed it. I am certain she didn't know about the kelp forest, as you no doubt do, having read Cedar's story earlier in this magnificent anthology.

scanning this way and that, his fear priming him for a hexcellent trick.

Kitty hid behind some bushes, pulled out her two ponytail holders, allowing her purple hair to fall over her face. She arranged her cat-eared hat on her head, and then popped up suddenly.

"*Aaoooooowww!*" Kitty howled.

"*Aaah!*" the farmer screamed. "*Aaah! Wolf!*"

Ha! She looked nothing like a wolf. Unless you were a frightened farmer afraid of meeting one. The Huntsman family lived nearby. That ought to get their attention.

Kitty disappeared and leaped through the forest, leaving no track for a Huntsman to follow. When she reentered the color-rich woods, she smelled human again, but not the farmer. No, it was surely Ashlynn Ella. Her scent was a mix of cypress tree, lily of the valley, lemon cleaning soap, and the crinkly paper that lines new shoe boxes.

Kitty climbed into a tree's canopy and watched for a time, finally spying Ashlynn running hither and thither and blither, coddling bunnies and consoling fawns and generally knee-deep in animal drama.

After sorting out several fauna issues, Ashlynn

seemed about to head home. Kitty snickered. If she could keep Cinderella's daughter busy in the woods, she'd have no time to finish her chores and pack for a new school year.

Invisible but for her hands, Kitty pinched a rabbit and blamed it on its sister, appeared suddenly to scare a fawn and again to tease a family of quail, and finally cupped a bird's nest out of a tree and placed it on the forest floor.

"Oh dear, I'll help you!" Ashlynn called out at the sounds of frightened, needy bleats and cheeps. "Don't worry, my little ones. Ashlynn will take care of you."

Kitty watched Ashlynn rush around, solving fuzzy, pawed, quivering-nosed drama. But then she caught a whiff of Hunter Huntsman—the scent of wood smoke, fir tree shavings, and soy turkey patties. Kitty wrinkled her nose and disappeared.[25]

Kitty fell down another wishing well. She climbed out into a rugged countryside. Here, the woods were ragged with wild, uplifted, crisscrossing limbs, as if

---

[25] It is curious that Kitty runs off before Hunter arrives. Is she afraid of Hunter? Does she sense that he, like she, is a predator, and so she must fight or flee his territory? Or perhaps she simply doesn't like the smell of soy turkey patties.

the trees had been frozen in the middle of casting a spell. In the distance, a black stone castle clung to a craggy cliff overlooking a wild, tossing sea.

An uncharacteristic shiver went galumphing down Kitty's spine.

She air-climbed up to a tower window and plunged through the wall. The inside was as dark as the outside, heavy velvet curtains shifting in invisible drafts, looming statues, alarming portraits. And within this exquisite gloom and grandeur, Kitty found Raven Queen.

Raven was sitting on the edge of her bed, dressed in shorts and a Tailor Quick T-shirt, one bare foot tucked up under her. On her guitar she was playing a song Kitty didn't know, but the tune slipped inside her, slick with sadness, and nestled below her heart, pressing up with a twinge and a hush. She felt as alone as a toad in a tree.

Kitty hesitated.

No tricks here, she told herself.

Cats have instincts, and Kitty knew—she just knew—that Raven would face plenty of riddles and snags and sticky-scratchy problems during her Legacy Year. Kitty wouldn't add to them. Not now.[26]

She left Queen Castle with a flick of her shadow feet, her arms out like a bird's wings, flying through the walls. The shadow statues stared. Kitty stuck out her tongue.

One more wishing well later, Kitty was expecting to pop up near yet another fancy palace or irritatingly adorable seaside village, but instead, there ahead of her towered Ever After High. She stood there (or more accurately, floated there), staring at the gray shadow of her school, and felt a strange, tickly, bubblish feeling wander beneath her ribs.[27] She tried to name it: excitement. Wait, was Kitty Cheshire actually excited about something?

Riddle-diculous! Absurdish! None-of-the-sense!

And yet those little bubbles of emotions kept rising and popping in her middle, making her smile feel real and a giggle threaten to escape her throat. Spying on so many of her classmates today

---

[26] I know. I'm as surprised as you are at Kitty's empathy and kindness. Kitty Cheshire, ever enigmatic.

[27] The feeling was so strong even Kitty couldn't conceal it from me.

made her feel closer to them, as if they'd all been holding hands and playing Duck Duck Dodo or something.

She almost, kind of, nearly admitted to herself that she'd missed them. Missed the oddly sensicle and prepostrasaurusly normal classmates of her school. Missed school, too.

Skipping hither and thither and quiver In-Between, Kitty watched Lizzie rush about, trying to create a home for her wobbly-nosed hedgehog but clearly needing a Wonderlandish place for herself.

How many times had Lizzie tried to grow a Wonderlandian plant in a planter in her dorm only to watch it wither? Like Lizzie herself (and Kitty, too, for that matter), the plants just didn't thrive far from Wonderland, especially not locked up indoors.

What Lizzie needed was an outdoors place. A bit of home. A garden. Of course, if Kitty tried to suggest that to Her Royal Highness the Princess of Hearts, Lizzie would just shout "Off with your head!" But maybe she could mislead her a bit into starting with a tiny Wonderland garden for hedgehogs....

Kitty spent some time searching the library for

just the right book. When Lizzie returned, Kitty disappeared and, making just her hand tangible, pushed the book off the shelf and onto Lizzie's shoe.

Kitty giggled, doing backflips through the silvery freedom of In-Between, and landing back where she'd been when Lizzie left hours ago as if she hadn't budged an inch.

She reappeared and smiled wide, her smile full of wonder. Her mother used to tell her, "Smile, Kitty. It makes people wonder if you're up to something."

"Kitty, have you been napping there this whole day?" Lizzie asked.

"More or less," said Kitty.[28]

Kitty Cheshire smiled for her mother and silently promised to always be up to something. Something wonder-ful.

No matter what, this was going to be a memorable year. [29]

---

[28] But definitely more. So, so much more.

[29] Whew! I did it! I believe this is the first-ever attempt to narrate Kitty Cheshire. And I have the scratch marks to prove it. Yes, somehow, even though I am a bodiless Narrator, whenever I got too close to her inner thoughts, Kitty managed to scratch me. Excuse me while I go search for some invisible ointment.

From the Storybook
(of Legends)
The Tale of Two Sisters

In *The Storybook of Legends*, Raven Queen faced the ultimate decision: to follow her mother's footsteps and become the next Evil Queen or break free from destiny and write her own future. In the Vault of Lost Tales, she discovered a spellbinding fairytale that helped her make her choice ... and changed her world forever after.

RAVEN TURNED THE BOOK OVER IN HER HANDS. The green leather cover was cracked and chipping, the pages yellow with age. She opened to the page marked with a ribbon. Her breath caught. "The Two Sisters."

ONCE UPON A TIME, THERE WERE TWO SISTERS. *One was so good and kind that butterflies were drawn to her. They perched on her fingers, touched her gently with their noses, and slept in her hair like jeweled pins. Although she was good-hearted,* her hair was dull and colorless, her cheeks without blush, her lips thin and sad. Her teeth pushed out and were as crooked as tumbledown fence posts.

Her sister, on the other hand, was as beautiful as a starry night. Her hair was deep black, her eyes twinkly, her teeth white behind her full-lipped smile. And yet she was so selfish and vain that wasps and flies were drawn to her. They buzzed around her head, landing in her hair to try to make their nests.

One morning their mother sent them to the well in the woods to fetch water. As they walked, the beautiful sister swatted at the bugs around her head.

"Shoo!" she said. "Shoo, you wretched things!"

The flies and wasps just kept buzzing.

"I'll show you," she said.

She climbed up the side of the well and put one foot in the bucket, holding on to the rope.

"Be useful for once and lower me down," she ordered her sister. "Make sure my head goes under, but then bring me back up quickly or I'll make you pay for my discomfort."

"As you ask, sister dear," said the ugly sister.

She lowered the bucket down. When the beautiful

sister's head went under the water, the wasps and flies flew away.

The ugly girl quickly pulled her sister back up. Her sister was much heavier than a bucket of water, and the rope hurt the girl's hands, but she didn't complain. She put out her hand and helped her beautiful sister out. But as soon as she was standing again, the beautiful sister shoved her away.

"That was too slow!" She shivered. The buzzing insects were gone at last, but she was soaked and freezing.

"Now it is your turn," the beautiful sister insisted. "I won't be the only one wet and cold."

"But I don't want to," said the ugly sister, holding a hand to her head. Butterflies with furled wings clung to her hair, fast asleep.

"Get in!" said the beautiful sister, pushing her toward the well.

The ugly sister was scared, but she climbed over the well's edge and put her foot in the bucket.

The beautiful sister lowered the ugly sister into the water.

The ugly sister kept her head up, straining to keep the butterflies above water.

"That's far enough," the ugly sister called as the water rose to her neck. "I'm all wet and cold now. You can bring me up." Water rose to her chin.

"All right, all right, you can stop yammering on," said the beautiful sister. She started to pull on the rope.

But she glanced down and saw her shadow lying on the forest floor. How sleek her neck! How fine her shoulders! How lovely her head without those wasps and flies flitting around. She raised her hands to smooth her hair and let go of the rope. She heard her sister cry out but was too interested in her silhouette to bother helping.

In the well, the ugly sister began to sink. She sank deeper and deeper into the cold water, the smooth sides of the well rushing past her fingers. She called out for her sister, but she heard no answer.

Her tears mixed with the well water. The butterflies drank it. And there, at the bottom of the well, a brilliant light flared. And another, and another, pink and white and blue, green and orange, dazzling shapes fluttering and flaring in the watery darkness. The wet butterflies, given power by the kind girl's tears, were glowing like fireflies and swimming like fish. The ugly sister drew courage from their light and swam, too. Together they fought their way up out of the well.

The ugly sister managed to seize the stones of the well and climb up the side. The glowing butterflies gripped her sleeves, helping to lift her over the side, and at last she put her feet down on the forest floor.

The beautiful sister forgot her shadow and looked up. The light from the butterflies became hotter and brighter. She shielded her eyes. There was a flash that knocked the selfish girl onto the ground.

When she could see again, her sister stood before her. Her hair was now the color of summer poppies, her eyes a brilliant leaf green, her cheeks pink as roses, her lips red as a hibiscus bloom. Her smile was breathtaking. She was as beautiful as she was kind.

"Oh no! What happened to you?" asked the kind sister.

The selfish sister's hands rose to her face. She raced to the well and looked at her reflection. All the shine and straightness was gone from her features. She was as unsightly now as her heart was unkind.

And from the depths of the well rose a swarm of

flies and wasps, very angry and louder than ever. The selfish sister ran and ran, through the woods and far away, but she could never escape that buzzing again.

The kind sister returned home with a bucket of water for her mother.

"Look what happened to my face," said the girl.

Her mother squinted. "What? You look the same to me as always."

The kind sister kissed her mother's cheek, and they lived happily together for the rest of their days.

Raven read the tale aloud to Maddie. And then she read the messages two people had jotted down in the margins of the pages.

I don't want to be the mean Beautiful Sister, and I don't want to drown my awesome little sister, Brutta, so I am not going to do it! Besides, she's not ugly and that's just mean to call someone that hateful word. We found a spell that will change our well into a portal. By the time anyone finds this note, we'll be long gone into another world where we're not forced to relive stupid stories.

That's right! Besides, like I'd ever let my sister drown my pet butterflies. I regularly whip her butt in Grimmnastics class.

You wish! I'll race you to the well!

ACKNOWLEDGMENTS

The world of Ever After was built on the shoulders of generations of authors, mythmakers, and narrators. Thanks to the most recent in that distinguished line of storytellers: the hexcellent team at Mattel, including Julia Phelps, Nicole Corse, Lara Dalian, Emily Kelly, Christine Kim, Robert Rudman, Ira Singerman, Audu Paden, and Venetia Davie. Pixie kisses and ogre handshakes to scrumdiddlyumptious Little, Brown Books for Young Readers, including Erin Stein, Andrew Smith, Melanie Chang, Victoria Stapleton, Christine Ma, Christina Quintero, Tim Hall, Mara Lander, Jenn Corcoran, and Renée Gelman. Cups of charm blossom tea for Barry Goldblatt, Deb Shapiro, and Tricia Ready. Dean Hale is a legendary hero in his own right whose apparent destiny is to collaborate with me in all our creations, from books to children. Thanks, honey.

ABOUT THE AUTHOR

New York Times bestselling author SHANNON HALE knew at age ten that it was her destiny to become a writer. She has quested deep into fairy tales in such enchanting books as *Ever After High: The Storybook of Legends*, *Ever After High: The Unfairest of Them All*, *Ever After High: A Wonderlandiful World*, *The Goose Girl*, *Book of a Thousand Days*, *Rapunzel's Revenge*, and Newbery Honor recipient *Princess Academy*. With the princely and valiant writer Dean Hale, Shannon coauthored four charming children, who are free to follow their own destinies. Just so long as they get to bed on time.

Turn the page for an
exclusive sneak peek at
the next chapter of

A new series by
acclaimed author
Suzanne Selfors
begins with
Next Top Villain.

To be born a fairytale princess is a blessing, indeed, but hers is not the lazy, carefree life that many imagine. There are numerous, important decisions that a princess must make every day.

For example, how would she like to be awoken in the morning? Should she choose an enchanted alarm clock to sing and dance around her bedroom? Perhaps her parents could employ fairies to gently sprinkle waking dust on her cheeks. Maybe she'd

prefer to have a household troll ring a gong or her MirrorPhone blare the latest hit song.

Duchess Swan, a fairytale princess proud and true, chose none of those options. Instead, she liked to be awoken by her favorite sound in the whole world.

Honk! Honk!

"Don't tell me it's morning already," a voice grumbled.

Duchess opened her eyes. While the honking had come from the large nest next to her bed, the complaining had come from across the room. To her constant dismay, Duchess did not sleep alone. This was the girls' dormitory at a very special school called Ever After High, and her roommate was Lizzie Hearts, daughter of the famously angry Queen of Hearts. Lizzie was not a *morning* person. Which is why she didn't own an alarm clock.

Honk! Honk!

"For the love of Wonderland!" Lizzie exclaimed, her voice partially muffled by a pillow. "Off with the duck's head!"

Duck? Duchess frowned. *Seriously?*

"Pirouette is *not* a duck," Duchess said, sitting up in bed. "Pirouette is a trumpeter swan."

"Duck, swan, pigeon…she's *loud*." Lizzie burrowed beneath a jumble of blankets.

"Of course she's loud," Duchess said. "She's named after a trumpet, not a flute."

Honk! Honk!

Duchess waved, to let Pirouette know that she hadn't gone unnoticed. Then Duchess pushed back the lavender silk comforter and set her bare feet on the stone floor. It was the first day of the new school chapter, and she was looking forward to her new classes. Why? Because each class was another opportunity to get a perfect grade. As a member of the Royals, Duchess took her princess duties very seriously. One of those duties was to be the best student she could be.

But there was another truth, somewhat darker and simmering below her perfect surface. Duchess Swan was well aware that grades were something

she could control, while her ill-fated destiny was not.

Tendrils of warm air wafted from the furnace vent, curling around her like a hug. She pointed her toes, then flexed, stretching the muscles. It was important to keep her feet limber, for she was a ballerina, and her feet were her instruments.

Honk! Honk!

"Okay. Hold your feathers." Duchess slid into her robe, then opened the window. A gust of fresh morning air blew across her face. Pirouette flew outside, heading for the lush green meadow. *A swan needs to stretch, too.*

Just as Duchess tied the laces on her dress, the bedroom door flew open and two princesses barged in. "Ever heard of a little thing called *knocking*?" Duchess asked.

"Can we talk?" the first princess said. Her name was Ashlynn Ella, daughter of the famously humble Cinderella. She yawned super-wide. "It's about your alarm clock."

The second princess, whose name was Apple White, daughter of the famously beautiful Snow White, also yawned. "Yes. Your goose alarm clock."

"She's not a goose." Duchess sighed. These princesses really knew how to get under her wings. "She's a swan."

"Oh, that's right. Sorry," Apple said.

The two princesses, having just rolled out of bed, looked unbelievably perfect. No bedhead, no sheet lines, no crusty sandman sand at the corners of their eyes. Apple was known as the Fairest One of All, and Ashlynn couldn't be any lovelier, even if she tried.

"Apple and I agree, as do the other princesses, that the honking sound that comes from your room every morning is starting to become a bit of a royal pain."

Royal pain? Duchess looked away for a brief moment so they wouldn't see the twinge of hurt feelings.

"I'd be happy to lend you some of my songbirds,"

Ashlynn said. Then she whistled. Three tiny birds flew through the doorway and landed on her outstretched finger. "It's such a cheerful way to wake up."

"Bird alarms aren't always reliable," Apple said. "I'd be happy to connect you to my network of dwarves. They'll send a wake-up call to your MirrorPhone."

"I don't need your songbirds or dwarves," Duchess told them, a bit annoyed.

Okay, she was more than a *bit* annoyed. Those girls were always acting as if they were better. They really ruffled her feathers!

Ashlynn, Apple, and Lizzie were Royals—the blood daughters of fairytale kings and queens. Being a Royal at Ever After High meant being part of the most popular and the most privileged group. Duchess was also a Royal, but she was different. Most Royals were destined to marry other Royals and rule kingdoms, living out their lives in comfort, health, and fortune. In other words, a big, fat Happily Ever After was waiting for most of them.

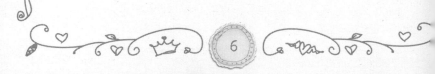

But Duchess did not have such a future, nor did she have a future as a dancer. Her destiny, as the daughter of the Swan Queen, was to turn into a swan and live out her days web-footed and feathered.

You can't perform a graceful *grand jeté* with webbed feet!

To make matters worse, she had no Happily Ever After with a charming prince written into her story.

Although Duchess's future did not seem fair, she'd accepted her circumstances. It was her duty to keep her story alive by fulfilling her destiny. She worked hard at her studies and her dancing. She did her best to make her family proud. But it drove her crazy that these girls had nothing more to worry about than being awoken by honking. It was just as Duchess often said: Birds of a feather flock together.

Lizzie popped her head out of the covers and glared at the intruders. "I order this meeting to be over. Now!"

"Sounds good to me," Duchess said. "Even though

I was so enjoying our little chat." She forced a smile. "However, it's time to get dressed for class. And you know what happens if you're late." She looked directly at Ashlynn.

"Oh my godmother, thanks for the reminder," Ashlynn said, her eyes widening with worry. If she was even just one second late, her clothes would turn into rags. She picked up the hem of her nightgown and rushed out the door, her songbirds following.

"Well, I'd better go, too. I hear my magic mirror calling. Charm you later," Apple said.

Duchess's smile collapsed the moment the princesses were gone. "Good riddance," she muttered under her breath.

"If my mother were here, she'd order their heads chopped off," Lizzie said. Then she burrowed back under the blankets.

Just as Duchess closed the bedroom door, Pirouette flew back in through the window. She landed at Duchess's feet, then turned the corners of her beak into a smile. Duchess knelt and gave her a hug. The wonderful scent of wind clung to Pirouette's white feathers. "Lucky girl," Duchess whispered. "You don't have to deal with know-it-all princesses."

Duchess filled a bowl with swan kibble—a mixture of breadcrumbs and grains—and set it on the floor. Pirouette began eating her breakfast. This was the calmest time of the day for Duchess, before the flurry of classes and activities, while Lizzie snored peacefully. And she usually began each day by writing in her journal.

She sat at her desk and opened the top drawer. There was no need to hide the golden book, because it was enchanted with a security spell. She pressed her fingers against the cover. A click sounded. This was the only place where she shared her truest of feelings—her darkest of secrets. After turning to a blank page, she dipped her quill into ink and began to write. But one thought filled her mind. One thought that never seemed to go away. And so she wrote:

> *I wish I had a Happily Ever After like Ashlynn's and Apple's.*

Then Duchess Swan looked out the window and sighed. Being a perfect princess meant she had to accept her destiny, even if that destiny was covered in feathers.

Ugly

Duckling

Duchess learned about her destiny on the morning after her eighth birthday, when she awoke and discovered that her feet had changed overnight.

It was a terrifying sight. "Grandma!" she cried. "What happened?"

Her grandmother pulled back the covers, took a peek, then sat calmly at the edge of the bed. "Dear child," she said. "This is the beginning."

"The beginning of what?" Duchess asked. She pulled her knees to her chest so she could get a

closer look. Her feet, which had been normal when she'd gone to sleep, were now flat, black, and webbed. "Take them off," she said, pulling on them as if they were shoes. "Make them go away!"

"They will go away," her grandmother said. "Don't worry. You will learn how to make them come and go as you please."

But they didn't go away. They stayed while she got dressed and they stayed while she ate breakfast. She tried to squeeze them into shoes, but they wouldn't fit. "I'm not going to school like this!" Duchess insisted.

"A princess must be educated," her grandmother said, gently pushing her out the palace door. "A princess must never be ashamed of who she is."

The village kids pointed and laughed as Duchess waddled down the lane, her big, flat feet making flapping sounds. "She looks like a duck," they said. "Ugly duck, ugly duck."

She felt ugly.

The webbed feet disappeared later that day. After

school, Duchess ran home, barefoot, and didn't complain about the sharp rocks in the lane. She was so happy to have toes again!

More changes came that year. She grew taller, her legs turning as skinny and gangly as a bird's. Sometimes when she laughed, she'd honk, which made all the other kids laugh. In the mornings, she'd find white feathers in her bed.

And she began to crave the plants that grew in the pond behind the schoolhouse. Spring green and tender, they looked so delectable. One day she waded in and began to eat them. "Look! The princess has flipped her crown. She's eating weeds!" Luckily, the village children didn't notice her also eating the little water bugs that skimmed the pond's surface. They tasted just as good as the cook's roasted beast.

What is happening to me?

Then, one morning, while walking home from school, Duchess spied a downy feather floating in the wind. It looked exactly like the feathers she

often found in her bed. She chased after it, then saw another, and another, drifting in the distance. The trail led her to the lake behind the palace, where a bevy of swans had gathered. Although they migrated to the palace grounds every winter, Duchess had never paid close attention to them. She knew that they were beautiful, with their snowy white feathers, black beaks, and black eyes. But as she sat in the grass, watching them preen and glide, she came to an amazing realization. Their swan feet looked exactly like the webbed feet she'd grown.

She was one of them!

And so, Duchess began to teach herself how to control the changes. It was not easy, for a sneeze could turn one arm into a wing, or a laughing fit could make a beak appear. By the time she was ten, she could control the transformation. She could turn herself into a swan whenever she wanted.

She saved this reveal for a special day at spell-ementary school. It was late spring and the class

was lined up along the edge of the swimming pool. "Today we will learn how to do a swan dive," her teacher, Mrs. Watersprite, said, pointing to the highest board. The students lined up at the bottom of the ladder. There were many trembling legs and terrified squeals as they climbed. "This is the most graceful dive of all," Mrs. Watersprite explained. "Put your hands above your head, lean forward, and jump! Then spread your arms wide, like wings."

One by one, the students jumped. Some clawed at the air as if trying to stop the fall. Some landed on their bellies. Others went feet first. "No, no, no!" Mrs. Watersprite hollered. "That was not graceful!"

Duchess went last. She raised her arms above her head and gripped the end of the board with her toes. It was a long way down. The other students looked small, some shivering beneath their towels. With their faces turned upward, they waited for the ugly duck girl to jump.

"Dive!" Mrs. Watersprite ordered.

Duchess bounced three times, then jumped. Just as gravity grabbed hold of her, she reached out her arms, closed her eyes, and transformed.

The dive was perfection. When she rose to the surface, the village kids cheered.

And that day, the ugly duck girl became the Swan Princess.

Read more about Duchess Swan and Lizzie Hearts in the new book coming soon!

And don't miss the companion Destiny Do-Over Diary!